The Great American Belly Dance

The Great American Belly Dance

DANIELA GIOSEFFI

DOUBLEDAY & COMPANY, INC., GARDEN CITY, NEW YORK
1977

"Dirty No-Gooder's Blues" by Bessie Smith © 1929 Frank Music Corp., 1350 Avenue of the Americas, New York, N.Y. 10019; © renewed 1957 Frank Music Corp. International copyright secured. All rights reserved. Used by permission.

"Belly Dancer," originally titled "Birth Dance, Belly Dancer," appeared in Ms. magazine, January 1976 issue, copyright © Daniela Gioseffi, 1975.

All the characters in this book are fictitious, and any resemblance to actual persons, living or dead, is purely coincidental.

ISBN: 0-385-13060-0
Library of Congress Catalog Card Number 77-72413
Copyright © 1977 by Daniela Gioseffi
ALL RIGHTS RESERVED
PRINTED IN THE UNITED STATES OF AMERICA
FIRST EDITION

*For my mother, Josephine, sisters Camille and Lucille,
and daughter Thea, as my poems have been for my father, Daniel.*

I acknowledge with gratitude my dear friends Joseph J. Morella, Richard J. Kearney, John Logan, Maurice Edwards, and E.S.Y. for their varied sustenance and encouragement. I thank my agent, Robert Datilla, friend Alice McIntyre, and editor at Doubleday, Susan A. Schwartz, for their advice and assistance.

CONTENTS

To recognize the truth: women own the earth, women own heaven, too—it is a tyranny without words—and without swords.

JACK KEROUAC

I understand the tree, it does not reason. . . . Fauns you have had your day: the poet now wants to talk to the tree.

JULES RENARD

The Woman-Soul leadeth us . . . on!

JOHANN VON GOETHE

STEP 1:

The Hip Bump

Dorissa Femfunelli saw the Mack truck approaching as she stepped out onto West Fifteenth Street. It was coming toward her with a greater velocity than any orgasm she had known. It was approaching like a butcher's knife ready to fall. She need only keep from resisting it. Open her legs and let it plow in. Give in to its brute force like a Sabine woman, Leda to the Swan, or a damsel to a dragon. Let it split her open like an obstetrician performing a Caesarean. Sweep her off her feet like no Prince Charming she had ever known. Take her away to death like a knight on a white charger. Accomplish its end with her. She would, at last, be completely ravished, the shattered pieces of a puzzle once a woman. A smorgasbord on asphalt.

She didn't want to look her rapist in the headlights. The *macho* truck might be discouraged from doing its job. She braced herself for the impact and lifted her eyes to a neon sign, greeting them from the other side of the street. In one split second, her life flashed before her as she read the writing on the wall:

1

BELLY DANCING LESSONS FOR BEGINNERS

The sign blinked off and on, lit by a fluorescence that glowed in daylight. To the right of it, a photograph of a bare-bellied, buxom woman smiled invitingly.

It was five o'clock in the afternoon, *a las cinco de la tarde,* when the bullring is covered with blood. She stepped back and suddenly decided to be reborn rather than bother with dying.

As she gripped her purse tightly to her side, like Joan of Arc her sword, she crossed the street and entered The Studio of Middle Eastern Dance. She had been divorced from Oliver Kelly for exactly three hours and forty-five minutes when she plunked down the last sixty dollars of her paycheck for belly dancing lessons.

Dorissa was a wife who had been undone—a parolee from the institution of marriage, one of the last of the daisies of the fifties to ride that "Bicycle Built for Two," or dream of frilly curtains, starched aprons, and Valentines. She was thirty-three, girlhood far behind her, with the painful loss of innocence that blocked Pandora's box before it was violated by the fickle Dick of fate. Now she would have to learn to live without Oliver. They would not finish out their lives watching each other's hair turn gray. It was not "to love, honor, and obey till death do us part" after all!

The next belly dancing class for beginners was not scheduled to start for more than an hour. The presiding dance instructress, an exotic-looking woman named Aneera Ohanian, accepted Dorissa's money, registering her name on a pink index card in a purple file box decorated with multicolored oriental designs. For future reference, she carefully inscribed Dorissa's measurements on the index card: height, 5 ft., 4½ in.; weight, 145 lbs.; 36-26-40.

Then advising Dorissa to relax and wait in the dressing room, Aneera Ohanian, in her long Moroccan robe, gracefully exited behind a tassled curtain that looked like the entrance to a Bedouin tent.

Dorissa stood in the glaring light of the dance studio dressing room and peered closely into the mirror at the tiny crow's-feet around her eyes. She gave her face a long, hard look, thinking how she'd changed since her wedding day. Reprimanding herself: "You've become dumpy and dull as dishwater!" she slowly began to undress in the silent cubicle, performing a strip-tease for her own benefit: She took off her Peck & Peck suit; white Misty Maiden slip; rubberized Lure-all girdle; stretch, Cross Your Heart, Cover Girl bra; and dark Show and Tell pantyhose. "Well," she told herself, turning this way and that and then standing naked body to naked image in the mirror, "Tell yourself a nice how-da-ya-do! You're thirty-three, no longer of the generation to be trusted. The last time you looked so closely into the mirror, you were seventeen, standing on your toes and dreaming of being a dancer like Isadora Duncan. Your breasts are still firm; your nipples still stick out like mountain peaks; but your belly has a Caesarean scar from navel to pubes; your shoulders sag; your face is still pretty, but your mouth droops; your eyes droop; your gorgeous auburn hair has become thinner and droops; even your knees droop. You've been a real droop for the past eight years, since you said, 'I do.' "

She stared deep into her own eyes in the dressing room mirror. "You're a fool and you'd better learn to love yourself and your body with its blood and bones and freckled nose and green eyes and too-pretty face and fat ass, mammary glands, battle-scarred belly, flatulence, armpit fuzz, pubic hair, and trouble-making cunt. I'll give you one year from today, and if you don't come to life, I'll finish you off, once and for all. Right to hell with a dump truck!" The tired, mirror image of her exchanged thoughts, muscle to muscle, bone to bone, pore to pore, capillary to capillary, crow's-foot to crow's-foot, belly to belly, with her body.

Turning from the mirror, she donned a red leotard and tights that Aneera had kindly lent her for her first lesson in belly dancing. The leotard fit her like a glove and exaggerated her bulges all the more.

"At least the color matches my bleeding heart better than my brown tweed suit," she thought. Leaving her well-cared-for brown tweed garment in a rumpled heap like a discarded snake skin, she took her horn-rimmed glasses from the bench and put them on. They were not very strong, but served to give her the proper image for a social-studies teacher at St. Aloysius School for Exceptional Children. Realizing the horn rims looked absurd with the flaming leotard, she took the glasses off, deposited them in her

3

black-leather purse, then snapped the purse shut like a coffin on a dead chapter of her life.

Now she was ready for her first lesson. She entered the studio where twelve women lolled on the floor, stretching themselves this way and that, in what appeared to be some sort of preparatory warmup. Dorissa thought how it looked like the class in natural childbirth she'd once tried to take. She shyly sat down upon the smooth floor and tried to look as if she knew what she was doing. Aneera Ohanian, a small, dark woman with long, black hair and wide-set eyes, entered the mirrored room.

"Okay, girls, let's start the warmups!" she said, stretching out on the floor in front of the group and proceeding to lead them in a series of dance exercises.

When Aneera finished the warmup exercises, which Dorissa executed with a great deal of stiffness, clumsiness, self-consciousness, and embarrassment, Aneera put on a cheerful, upbeat Turkish tune and began to lead her students around the room. They followed in a line vaguely reminiscent of the circus parade in Fellini's 8½. Women of every age, strange shape, and size followed Aneera around the room, with Dorissa awkwardly taking up the rear.

With right toe pointed, step out on one foot and, before actually accepting your weight onto it, bump your hip to the side. Repeat with left side. Continue, alternating. Right foot: Step, point, bump, pause. Left foot: Step, point, bump, pause.

Although Dorissa felt ridiculous for the first few turns around the room, she followed the procession, bumping when she should have stepped and pointing when she should have bumped. With Aneera's constant vocal encouragement, Dorissa soon gained enough confidence to keep up with the others.

Step, point, bump, pause. Step, point, bump, pause.

4

STEP 2:

Hip Circles

Aneera Ohanian had warned Dorissa to take it easy, but Dorissa pursued her course as if chased by Furies. Against Aneera's advice, she registered herself in every morning, noon, and nighttime class available at the studio.

"I want to learn as quickly as possible," insisted Dorissa, with a maniacal expression.

Aneera decided that Dorissa was a bit of a basket case. She feared that the peculiarly insistent Dorissa would destroy every muscle in her body by exercising it to death, but Dorissa's will triumphed. She grew muscular control like fruit from blossoms. In two and a half superhuman weeks, she became one of the best dancers among the hundred or so of Aneera's students. Plump though she was, Dorissa could glide, dip, and shimmy her way through all the basic steps of the belly dance while keeping a rhythm with her finger cymbals. Of course, Aneera didn't know that when not in class, Dorissa was dancing ceaselessly, every wak-

5

ing moment, until she fell into a stupor—a sleep that nothing but the rhythms of Middle Eastern music could penetrate.

Without the slightest realization of what she was doing, Dorissa had invented her own after-the-divorce belly-dance therapy. There was no time to moon gloomily about how romantic love fails, how she was not Elvira Madigan, Juliet, or Isolde, or even Snow White, Cinderella, or Rapunzel, how Lancelot doesn't really rescue Guinevere. She danced and, after a bit of food, or a belch, or a movement of her bowels, she danced some more. On and on. She didn't see anyone; she didn't hear anyone's voice except Aneera's. She shut out the world like a psychotic and danced until her body was the only reality she knew.

She didn't go in to work or bother to report in sick at St. Aloysius School for Exceptional Children. She didn't even call to say she was quitting her job. She just danced as though dance were a death that would bring her to life again—clumsily at first, and then like an ugly duckling, transforming into a swan. She coaxed and cajoled her muscles into responding. She went beyond endurance, pushing, stretching, and rolling every pain in her heart out through her sweating pores. A whole new, exciting career in the mysterious blue-lit cafes of New York bubbled in her fantasies.

Since the afternoon two and a half weeks earlier when they'd signed their divorce papers, Oliver hadn't been able to reach Dorissa. She had not yet installed a telephone in her apartment. Whenever he traveled down from the Upper West Side of town to ring her doorbell, she wasn't home. His mother had been hounding him to check on Dorissa to see that she was all right. Her boss had called him several times. Oliver had finally resorted to calling the police to locate his missing ex-mate, but every time the police went by to look for Dorissa, she was out, attending one of her dance classes.

Finally, Oliver, escorted by a police detective, went to Dorissa's apartment one evening, to hear Middle Eastern music blaring inside the door. When she didn't answer, after several rings of her buzzer, they broke in the door and found her dancing-whirling in a naked frenzy, breasts bobbing, buttocks shimmying, to loud music. Oliver politely wrapped Dorissa in his raincoat, and with

6

profuse apologies, dismissed the police detective. After the policeman departed, he turned with a vengence toward Dorissa.

"Are you mad?" he shouted. "Your father, your boss, your daughter, and my mother have been worried out of their minds."

"Did they cry as much as they would have at my funeral?" she spat back at him.

"What in the hell is wrong with you, Dorissa? Have you no sense of responsibility? Chrysta has been asking for you every day. How much longer do you want my mother to keep her?" When Dorissa didn't answer him, but kept on shimmying as if to some internal rhythm, Oliver grabbed her by the shoulders and shook her.

"What are you doing, Dora?" he sighed in despair.

"I'm learning to belly dance, and it's none of your business anymore what I do!" she declared flatly.

"Belly dance! What for?" asked Oliver in astonishment.

"Because I *feel* like it. I'm giving up teaching!" she announced, surprised to hear herself say so. "I'm going to look for a job dancing!"

"You . . . ? A belly dancer? Dorissa, don't be ridiculous! Anyway . . . you're too fat!"

"What do you know about it, Oliver? A belly dancer has to have a belly!"

"What about your Caesarean scar?" reasoned Oliver, trying to bring her to her senses.

"I'll paste jewels over it. Who cares? Get out of here and leave me alone." With the word "alone," her face broke like a chandelier, and tears fell from her eyes like shattered crystal onto the bare floor of the unfurnished apartment.

Dorissa for the first time lashed out savagely at Oliver. "You sure wanted me to dance at your senior prom, ten years ago! You were such a coward! You wanted me to rock 'n' roll and twist myself into an abortion."

Oliver, controlling his rage, spoke calmly, grabbing hold of Dorissa's wrists as her arms flew in his face. "You were scared your father would find out you were pregnant." Having secured her arms, he continued in a rational tone, "I had no money! And two

7

years of graduate scholarship that could've gone down the drain! As it was, my thesis took forever to finish!"

"Your thesis!" Infuriated all the more by his patronizing attitude, she tried to struggle free. "Who wrote and typed your thesis, Oliver? Who sat up nights sorting your research notes? I probably know more about the implications of Kirlian photography on the study of photosynthesis in nonflowering plants than you, Professor!" she jeered.

"Don't get hysterical, Dora! You loved every minute of it. You carried on as if you were Mrs. Semyon Kirlian, herself! You thought you were Madame Curie!" he mocked.

"You've always hated me for being better at writing your thesis than you were, Oliver. Admit it!" she shrieked, nearly pushing him over in her rage. "You wanted me to mother you. Then you hated me for doing it. And don't tell me I'm hysterical! You haven't an emotional brain in your body. Let go of me!" She tried to bite his hands, which still gripped her wrists. They struggled and the tall, clothed Oliver rolled on top of the short, naked Dorissa, pinning her to the floor.

"You're hurting me!" she cried.

"I'll let you go as soon as you calm down! You're behaving like a maniac."

Dorissa was wild with rage. She pushed him off and ran to the other side of the room. With sheer adrenaline force, she hurled a plantless flower pot full of soil that fell prey to her outrage, in Oliver's direction.

"You're the one who messed up our marriage by fucking around with your mousey students! Biology 101. The dean should have known your curriculum!" she bellowed.

The flower pot missed Oliver's head, smashing to pieces on the wooden floor. He was dazed. Finally, he stormed over to her and slapped her squarely across the face. "You could have killed me with that thing!"

She whimpered and fell back against the wall. After several large involutionary gasps and sighs, she was silent, staring at the floor.

He felt guilty for having slapped her. She looked pathetic stand-

8

ing, emotionally exhausted, nude in his open raincoat, against the bare wall—staring with glazed eyes at the floor.

He cleared his throat. "Well, it didn't take you long to get even, Dora. What about that visiting lecturer at St. Aloysius, that weird professor of comparative theology, that you screwed behind the altar of the chapel? Because you were so pissed off at me. Instead of understanding that I was driven to rediscover my youth!"

After a long pause, she sank down against the wall. Her voice was dull and lifeless. "How could I understand that, Oliver? I've never discovered my own!"

Her lifelessness stimulated more guilt in him. He tried once again to prod her into action. "Well, I never wanted to get married in the first place. Why did you have to go and confound biological science by getting pregnant on birth-control pills?" He nervously smoothed out the rumples in his brown corduroy suit, dusting soil from the shattered flower pot off his pantcuffs.

Without moving or lifting her gaze, she spoke in a soft, dejected voice. "Oliver, how come you've always acted like you had nothing to do with making me pregnant? Chrysta was your conception as much as mine. And so was the child I had aborted before her, when I was still an innocent college girl. I've been thinking since I saw you so smug and complacent, signing those papers in the lawyer's office. I was crying so much I couldn't even see the dotted line, but you . . ." She paused to control her emotions. "Nine years, the best years of my life, and they all meant nothing to you!"

Oliver didn't want to listen. "Dorissa, it's over. It's done. We're divorced, and the divorce was your idea more than mine."

She continued quietly, never lifting her eyes from the floor, never moving a muscle, just leaning against the wall like a rag doll devoid of its frock. "I was thinking, Oliver, about how we met, when we were working nights at the Venetian Palace Restaurant. Remember? In between customers, you used to sneak meatballs and tortoni from the kitchen and serve them to me in the back of the checkroom. You were always interrupting my homework with that phony Italian accent you faked to get bigger tips. Then, after you'd won and had me, if I interrupted your homework in the back of the kitchen, you got furious. You seem to have forgotten

9

all the spumoni and furtive feels you plied me with behind the coatracks, Oliver. I was just a dumb little college girl when you met me." For a moment, visions of spring, youth, and maiden-hood danced in her head, relieving her agony, as she sat looking defeated.

She caused guilt to well up in him, then compensatory anger. "Look, Dorissa, why are you bringing all this up now, *after* the divorce? You were no innocent girl when I met you." He lashed out at her. "You had already been fucking around with Salvatore Carboratore, and your father's rich old friend, James Honeywell!"

Stung by his words, she stared glassy-eyed at her cheap stereo, purchased on credit two weeks before. In the silence, its needle creaked around the finished record. "I met Salvatore just before I met you. He was the first boy I ever dated. He lived across the street. Our addresses were the only thing we had in common. He was always standing there at the curb, with his muscles bulging, polishing the headlights on his convertible. It took him a year to get me to go for a ride in that immaculate machine! And months to get me into the back seat. Even then, I couldn't do it. I was so nervous and scared. Either my hymen was very tough, or he was very clumsy. I thought I had a bone in the wrong place. I thought I was some kind of abnormal freak. My God, was I a virgin! I didn't know what I had down there. The misery I went through, afraid to ask my parents about anything. My father would have killed me, and my mother thought sex was the dirtiest thing on earth!"

"Oh come on, Dorissa. You slept with him, didn't you?" He had lost all patience.

"If that's what you want to call it. When Salvatore's mother was at church saying novenas for his father, he tempted me into his bedroom to show me his football pendants. Once he got me out of the back seat and into his bed, he managed to break through. I was glad to find out I didn't have a bone there, after all, but terrified to have lost my virginity. When Salvatore started going steady with the gas station owner's daughter, because he liked to use her father's carlift to work on his rebuilt Chevy, I thought I'd die. I was sure no other man would ever want to marry me because I wasn't a virgin anymore. I was reading *The*

Decline and Fall of the Roman Empire in the checkroom when you interrupted me, *Oliver Kelly!* You drove me crazy with your phony Italian accent and got me pregnant in the front seat of your old beat-up Ford. I was so glad that you weren't crazy about cars! You were so handsome, Oliver. I can still remember the night it happened."

"Dorissa, will you stop this insane reminiscing. It all happened over ten years ago! You're sitting there in your birthday suit. It's ridiculous!" He turned away and lit his pipe as if ignoring her. "Get dressed and give me my raincoat!"

She got up from the floor and took him by the arm, laughing to goad him into listening. "It was the first snowfall of winter. I was so tired from checking heavy mink coats all night and studying for my exams in between customers. You drove me home from work. I loved you so much, Oliver. I would have done anything for you. 'Earth Angel,' by the Platters were playing on your car radio. You told me I was your Earth Angel. When you put your hand in my sweater, I almost fainted. I thought you were my knight in shining armor! I wanted to marry you and live happily ever after!"

He pulled away from her and crossed the room with the excuse of lifting the stereo's needle from the end of the record. "No wonder you couldn't hear me banging on your door, this thing was so loud! Where did you get this piece of junk?"

She followed him across the room. "I was terrified when I found out I was pregnant. I was ready to commit suicide! My father would have had another heart attack if he found out. My mother would have cried for months. And you acted like I got pregnant to trap you into marriage!"

"Well, I wasn't the only one you were fucking around with. James Honeywell was on the scene, always flying in and taking you to the city for tourist treats! I figured you were more sophisticated and knew what you were doing!"

"Oh Oliver, how could you talk that way? You know very well that Uncle Jimmy was an old friend of the family. He was the only rich person my family ever knew firsthand. They were very impressed with his showy presents. He and my father fought in the war together before he struck it rich! My father trusted him. I was an inexperienced girl, and he took advantage of me! He got me drunk for the first time in my life and raped me in the Astor Hotel, only months before I met you. I was scared to tell my parents about it. The only other time I ever slept with him was to get him to take me down South for the abortion *you* made me face all alone. It was your child, and you know it. I should never have had to face the whole thing without your help. Some biology student you were! Thinking I could douche a baby away!"

"Look, Dorissa, I was an Irish Catholic boy and pretty innocent myself! At least you didn't have to spend your youth in parochial schools getting told your dick would fall off if you masturbated! And it's not my fault your father was too trusting to suspect your Uncle Jimmy of being an old letch! Now let's stop talking about this. Get down to why you are carrying on, now, belly dancing like a maniac!"

"You've been hanging around your little liberated students so much, you've forgotten what it was like for women of my generation. My father lived by the patriarchal double standard. My pituitary gland wasn't supposed to whisper any longings to my gonads! I was supposed to hold it all in and never go below the waist! Remember, Oliver, Uncle Jimmy came in very handy when you wanted me to ask him to get me an abortion. You should have been there with me in that Texas motel while I was bleeding my guts out! I thought I was going to die. The plaster statue of the Virgin Mary that my Aunt Lizabetta used to pray to just before she died in childbirth haunted me in that room. I kept thinking of Mary's Immaculate Conception and feeling dirty! That statue appeared to me in my sleep, for years! I felt so guilty for killing my baby! I still feel guilty. I keep thinking it was probably a son like my father always wanted. You've always made me feel that my pregnancy was all my fault. How could you have let me go through that horrible abortion all by myself?"

"Well, what did you want from me? I still had two years of school to finish, and a scholarship I would have to forfeit. My parents would have had a fit if I'd married you because you were pregnant!" He paced about impatiently. "Get your robe and give me my raincoat or I'll leave without it!"

She ignored his threat. "You know something I've never told you, Oliver, because I was too ashamed: Uncle Jimmy introduced me to the sheriff of his county. The sheriff felt me up and drove me to the local abortionist, who was his mistress. She was an ex-nurse who was an old letch, too. She kept pinching me and telling me what cute breasts and legs I had. Everybody got in their greedy pinches, including Uncle Jimmy. All he did to help when I was scared and crying was offer me a Nieman Marcus bikini, a black one with rhinestones! All the while, you were sitting at home, cozy, studying for your exams, I was practically bleeding to death and missing mine! I realized that just yesterday!"

"Dorissa, for the last time, stop it! What has all this got to do with you belly dancing like a maniac?"

She returned the needle to the beginning of the record and pushed the volume up full blast. "I'm dancing because it makes me feel good. I'm learning to accept and enjoy this body of mine, which has gotten me into so much trouble and agony, partly thanks to you, Oliver! It's about time I started having some fun with my body!" She flung Oliver's raincoat in his face and began to dance in naked seduction before him.

"Stop that! You look lewd!" he shouted angrily, taking the needle off the record again.

"This is my house, Oliver, not yours! If you don't want to face the music, just get out!" She tried to put the needle back on the record, but he restrained her hand.

"I've known you to plunk your money down for exotic dancers, Oliver! Aren't ex-wives supposed to be sexy?" She ran to the door and stepped naked into the hall. "If you won't get out of here, I will."

With his usual sense of mortified respectability, Oliver bounded after her, pulled her inside, and slammed the door shut.

"Are you stark, raving mad? What kind of a nut are you? I should've fought you for custody of Chrysta. She'd be better off with me."

"You never wanted her in the beginning, Oliver. It was only after you realized that she was keeping you out of Vietnam that you started enjoying the idea of a child. I went through that emergency Caesarean all by myself, just like the abortion, without any help from you, and it was more like being on the front lines than you've ever been. You should've been there in that motel holding my hand, instead of Uncle Jimmy handing out Nieman Marcus swimsuits to get in his furtive feels."

"Well, he was your father's friend, not mine!" he said, avoiding her gaze. "You're the one who asked him for help!"

"Because the only solution you came up with was that expanding douche bag that exploded in my face!"

"Well, I was just a kid, too. Your mother should have told you about those things. I shouldn't have had to buy you a douche bag!"

"My gynecologist told me that douching is not necessary. It kills the proper pH. It's just that you're so uptight about a woman's natural odor. You are still a lousy biology student!"

"My God, Dorissa, I've never heard you talk like this before. I think you've been under too much strain. Besides, 'to douche or not to douche' is not the subject of this conversation!" He was beside himself. "I think you ought to see a psychiatrist! You're behaving very peculiarly. Maybe you need some help."

He frightened her. She started to cry, but to cover it up, she laughed and changed the subject. "Did I tell you about the time my mother found my father's pornography collection in the basement, when he was in the hospital last winter?"

"Your family always was a little crazy!"

"At least we let it all hang out. We didn't hold it all in and get ulcers like yours. Your father repressed your feelings right out of existence!" She sank down on the floor and hugged her bare knees to her naked breasts. "I think I've been carrying on to get some kind of a rise out of you, Oliver. Your control, your reserve, make me want to scream. You were so rational in the lawyer's office. So logical and proper! The best years of my life meant nothing to you."

Oliver changed the subject, trying not to notice her nakedness. "You mean your father had a pornography collection the whole time he was lecturing me about bringing you home before midnight?"

"That double standard is not too unusual, Oliver. You're into it yourself."

"What did your mother do?" He was laughing at the irony. She realized that she was still attracted to his face when it softened.

She'd never been able to get him to cry, but she'd made him laugh, if not as often as she'd driven him to anger.

"My mother was so shocked when she found photographs of naked women behind her washing machine that she called him in the hospital and told him he deserved to die for having such a filthy mind. The poor old man." She groaned and lay back on the floor and held her stomach.

"Maybe your frigid mother was what made you so frigid after a while." Oliver tried not to notice how her crotch was open before him.

"You are what made me frigid, Oliver." Tears glistened in her red eyes.

"Here, let me help you relax," he said, taking her in his arms and touching her breasts.

She felt his warmth. She hadn't been close to another human being for many days. Oliver's familiar smell and touch were comforting. She began to breathe deeply. Her body released some of its anxiety.

"I know I won't ever be free of you until I'm free of resentment toward you, Oliver."

Oliver began to kiss and suck on Dorissa's breasts. She sighed deeply. They sank all the way down onto the floor and made love. Then they fell asleep in an exhausted heap.

At five o'clock the next morning, waking up stiff, and opening her eyes directly into Oliver's sleeping, snoring face, she felt a tremendous, uncontrollable rage. She staggered into the bathroom and found her Enchanting Lady, portable, expanding douche bag. It was the same kind of rubber balloonlike contraption Oliver had given her years before. She filled the nozzle of the balloonlike bag with cold water until it was swollen and very near to bursting. Then she carried it out to where Oliver lay snoring. Holding it in one hand just above his face, she smacked it hard with the other, the way children pop a paper bag filled with air to hear it explode with a bang.

"Good morning, Oliver. It's about time you woke up," said Dorissa with a great deal of peaceful satisfaction. "I've got a lot of dancing to do, and you're cluttering up my floor." Then she turned on her music and began to practice the Basic Hip-circle.

Stand erect, feet almost together, knees slightly flexed. Pivot the middle of the body around the base of the legs, allowing the hips to inscribe a circle drawn parallel with the floor, the same way as a hula hoop might. Now try your hip circles in time with different Middle Eastern tempos, until you can move your hips around in the smoothest circle possible.

STEP 3:

The Belly Roll

Dorissa stopped dancing and looked down at the broken pieces of blue rubber lying around on the floor. Oliver as always had managed to spoil her fun, to find the chink in her armor and thrust in his lance. She went into the bathroom and stood naked before the mirror on the back of the bathroom door. Her skin glistened with the sweat of dancing. The strenuous exercise had cleared her head; she felt high, as if on drugs. She stared at herself as she had the first day she stood naked in front of the dance studio mirror. She realized that her posture was more erect. Her stomach wasn't sticking out quite as much, and her shoulders slouched less. Her face glowed, and the circles under her eyes were gone. Her knees didn't droop. Neither did her mouth.

The morning sun, just rising over the city, penetrated the skylight above and filtered over her in rays of light, streaking across her belly, spotlighting her navel. She found herself thinking how she once breathed through that eye in the middle of her belly, attached to her mother, Sophia. She thought how Chrysta once breathed inside her. She began to undulate her belly as best she could, rolling it up and down as Aneera had taught her to.

With the explosion of cold water in his face, Oliver had totally lost his cool and called her a "crazy stripper" for learning to belly dance. "Burlesque queen, go-go girl, slut," were a few of the insults he'd hurled at her in the course of his angry tirade.

"Aneera called it an *art*," recalled Dorissa, as she gazed into her magic navel eye in the mirror. She resolved to look up an article on belly dancing that Aneera had mentioned in class. In her purse was a crumpled piece of paper on which she had scribbled "*Dance Perspectives*, issue No. 10, Lincoln Center Library, Dance Research Division.

Bounding into the living room, she began picking up the pieces of broken douche bag and found several dollars in cash, money Oliver had lent her when she pleaded poverty. He had folded the bills into a rectangle and thrust them into her cleavage.

"Here, sexy Sadie!" he had mocked. Then he had stomped out.

After picking up the money, Dorissa dressed and headed for the supermarket. She meant to buy some fruit and vegetables, but in the produce department she saw a sign with a photo of a gorgeous brunette, cleavage displayed, holding a bowl of ivy to her breast and smiling invitingly.

BRIGHTEN YOUR LIVING ROOM WITH GREENERY
HOUSE PLANTS: HALF PRICE

Dorissa was moved by the fact that many of the plants were withered and in need of a home. She used all the money she had and bought seven of them, then carted them back to her apartment and arranged them around the unfurnished living room. They looked at home alongside her Avocado Tree.

She and Chrysta had planted the Avocado together and brought it up from a pit of one they'd eaten for lunch. The little Tree's leaves were turning quite brown at the edges. Dorissa carefully picked the dead leaves from it. Looking at the little green Tree reminded Dorissa that she hadn't seen Chrysta in nearly three weeks. Dorissa felt pangs of guilt and sadness.

Later that day, she found herself in the Dance Research Division of the Lincoln Center Library of the Performing Arts. Her green eyes were lowered behind the pink-tinted lenses of her new aviator glasses, bought just a few days before. She had responded to a sign in an optician's window, which bore a gorgeous eyeglassed redhead, cleavage exposed, smiling invitingly.

CHANGE YOUR IMAGE TO YOUTHFUL AND LOOK AT THE WORLD THROUGH ROSE-COLORED GLASSES

Dorissa, looking more youthful than she had a couple of weeks earlier, read the rose-colored pages spread out before her:

The seeker after knowledge in the East will often come upon conflicting opinions regarding the origins of the ancient dance of the stomach. It is generally agreed, however, that the cafe belly dance, performed in modern cities all over the world, is of ritualistic origin. Descended from one of the oldest dances in the world, its belly-rolling contractions are imitations of childbirth contractions. Once a primitive therapy dance, it was meant to insure the strength and agility of the female torso for childbirth and was performed as a fertility rite.

She was thrilled to find that the dance that so attracted her, the dance that Oliver had equated with burlesque, was, indeed, an ancient folk art. The idea of the belly rolls being imitations of birth contractions intrigued her. She herself had never known the experience of natural childbirth, she had been rushed to the hospital for an emergency Caesarean. She'd felt like Gulliver at the mercy of the Lilliputians, strapped down with her private parts displayed for the masked creatures who surrounded her as they prepared to operate. A screen was placed in front of her belly, over her chest, but she could view the distorted reflection of the proceedings in the operating lamp above. Its shiny chrome reflected the elfish, masked doctors as they painted her bulging abdomen with an orange-colored fluid and then made the incision.

All she remembered was a baby's cry and the sight of the small, wet body lifted above the screen that separated her from her lower self. She saw the iridescent umbilicus. When she awoke in the recovery room, her stomach felt like pieces of broken glass has been jabbed into it. There were moaning women lying all around her. They writhed and groaned for help, as if in Dante's Inferno.

"How was it? Much easier that way, I bet," said Oliver, being excessively cheerful as she tried to see him through the blurred vision.

"Oliver," she answered in a doped fit of anger, "it made me wish I had never met you." Then she fell into an exhausted sleep. When she awoke the next day, her stomach was afire with her contracting uterus. She burned with fever, but when she insisted on summoning her doctor from his office, he accused her of being "hysterical and belligerent."

"I saw you earlier this morning, Mrs. Kelly! Stop acting like a child! You're fine," he repeated and hung up.

Later, he was chagrined to discover that Dorissa had puerperal fever. Only massive doses of antibiotics saved her from succumbing to the disease that had taken so many lives of women down through the centuries, before doctors discovered that the contaminating germs of their own hands were the cause of childbed fever. The hospital hushed up the twentieth-century blunder.

It was a long and tedious recovery. When she'd entered the hospital, the trees were bare. As she emerged, one rainy day in early spring, they were lush, full, wet, and hanging with fresh, green leaves. She was glad to be alive and to have her baby in her arms at last. For a long time she was exceedingly aware of the bright colors and sounds and smells of the good things of the earth around her.

———◆———

As she stood in the stacks of the dance research library, intrigued by her reading, Dorissa began to roll her belly as Aneera had taught her to see if it felt like a woman about to deliver. A young man who was standing behind her in the aisle was puzzled to feel her undulating bottom tapping and gliding against his. Deciding it was an invitation, he turned around to lay a hand on her buttock, just as she hurried down the aisle with an armload of books. Dorissa read long into the afternoon and early evening and arrived at Aneera's studio a few minutes after her lesson had begun.

"Tonight, ladies, we will work on the Belly Roll, or Arch and Contraction," Aneera explained. "It's probably the most difficult of belly dancing steps, but it is absolutely central to the dance as performed in Egypt, Turkey, Greece, Israel, or any Middle Eastern country."

Dorissa watched her teacher with respectful admiration as she tried to perfect her own belly roll.

Stand erect, feet comfortably apart, knees slightly flexed. Pull in your stomach, just under the rib cage, so that your back is slightly rounded. Then push out your LOWER abdomen as far as you can, so that your back arches a little. The muscular movement should roll smoothly down the belly as the back rounds and arches. After a good deal of practice, you will begin to imitate a smooth and voluntary birth contraction, just like the one that pushed you, head first, into this world, where, if you are a woman, you can be reborn learning to belly dance.

As she practiced rolling and flexing her stomach before the studio mirror, Dorissa, who'd been an ardent social studies student, remembered what she'd read in the library. One Asian had written of the dance as a poem of the mystery and pain of motherhood, primitive purity, representing maternity, the mysterious conception of life, the suffering and joy with which a new soul is brought into the world.

In early civilization, Dorissa had read, men didn't know what part they played in conception. As a result, women were worshiped as divine deliverers, fertility goddesses whose moony wombs waxed and waned, bleeding rhythmically in lunar cycles.

The information she'd devoured all afternoon ran through her mind, making her view Aneera as some pagan priestess of the moon goddess Diana, teaching a chorus of dancers to perform sacred rites.

21

For the first time, Dorissa looked around the class and studied the bodies and faces of the other students. To the right of her, a tall, slender platinum blonde with a highly teased hairdo chewed gum in rhythm with her abdominal movements. The blonde paused to flutter her false eyelashes and giggle.

"Oh Jesus, I can't get it right. It doesn't feel *natural* to me. I feel silly sticking out my stomach after all these years of paying Playtex to hold it in. It's sexy as hell, though, ain't it?" she concluded.

An overweight, middle-aged woman with short, brown, close-cropped hair and sad, dull eyes stood to the left of Dorissa. The woman succeeded only in sucking in her rounded middle and pushing it out again with a jerk. "Oh God, I can't do it either," she groaned. "I feel silly. But I bet it makes me lose weight."

Both women were beginners. Another beginner, wearing horn-rimmed glasses, her long hair in a knot at the back of her neck, stood behind Dorissa. The beginner was able to execute the stomach roll efficiently enough, but her movements were stiff and confined. Neither too fat nor too thin, she appeared the stereotype of a small-town librarian, neatly shaped, but neither proud nor sensual—capable of moderate muscular activity, without any sense of style or grace.

Suddenly Dorissa felt profound empathy with the women surrounding her in the mirrored wall. She wanted to take each one of them by the hand and make them feel alive, desirable, healthy, proud, necessary, good.

Glad the class was ended, she put her clothes on in an isolated corner of the dressing room, as the other women chattered of husbands, families, children.

Hearing that Aneera was dancing at the Phoenician Garden on Eighth Avenue that night, Dorissa felt the need to do a little firsthand fieldwork. The only belly dancers she'd ever seen were Cecil B. DeMille creations. Aneera would be authentic and live.

Dorissa rushed home, showered, put on her basic black dress, and looked in the mirror. The dress sagged a little where she'd eliminated a few pounds. It was too long and looked frumpy.

"I dare you to go to the cafe all alone!" she challenged herself.

She began to apply her make-up but recalled how the tall, heavily made-up blonde in her dance class giggled and decided that her inept stomach contractions were "sexy."

Suddenly Dorissa tossed her make-up purse, full of Coral Gloss Burnt-coral Blusher, Midnight-black Eyeliner, Blue-eye-allure, Thick-lash Mascara, and Translucent Face Powder into the bathroom wastebasket. It joined the blue rubber remains of her Enchanting Lady portable, expanding douche bag. She picked up her purse and scurried out of the apartment.

——————◆——————

"Sorry, miss, we don't have a table for one!" explained the headwaiter at the Phoenician Garden as he greeted Dorissa at the door. "*Women* don't usually come here *alone*. We're crowded on Friday nights."

"But I want to stay and watch the dancer; she's my teacher. May I stand at the bar?"

"No, sweetheart, not unless you want to meet a few of our customers." He indicated a bunch of loud-talking, cigarette-smoking men who were leaning against the bar, drinks in hand. "Well, honey, the only thing I can do is ask the fellow over there if you can share his table for two. He's supposed to have someone join him, but she hasn't shown up."

The anxious Dorissa didn't want to sit with a stranger, but she realized there was no alternative. It was the first time, since she'd married, that she'd gone out in the evening by herself.

She imagined herself coming onto the stage of the cafe. Oliver sat before her in the audience. She was dressed in a gorgeous gold-and-silver belly dancing costume, glittering with elegance. Oliver rushed to the stage and fell on his knees before her.

"Please come back to me. You're so beautiful. I've been a fool!" he entreated. She pushed him aside, with her tanned, bare leg showing through the slit in a long chiffon skirt.

"Not now, Oliver," she said. "I'm busy." Then she began to dance as a wild cheer went up from the crowd around her.

Suddenly the daydream changed. She was standing in the fluorescent light of a bathroom with her hair in curlers. Oliver stood before her, his face angry and dripping with water.

"Goddamn it, Dora, you forgot to turn off the shower nozzle

23

again. Every time I go to fill the tub with water, I get a shock of cold water on my head."

The headwaiter interrupted her reveries.

"Well," he said as he returned to his station, "you can share the table with that guy over there. That's the best I can do for you, sweetheart! Next time bring your boyfriend."

Dorissa hesitated, then walked boldly over to the table where a dark-haired man was eating a Greek spinach pie. She excused herself, turned her chair sideways toward the dance floor, and sat down.

"I'm studying dancing and I just want to watch the dancers," she blurted out as if intimidated into offering an explanation.

"It's perfectly all right with me if you want to sit here," he answered accommodatingly, looking up and carefully blotting his lips with his napkin. She noticed that the man was rather pleasant-looking. He was neatly dressed in a black pinstripe suit, white shirt, and dark-blue tie, and seemed about forty-five, or more. Though his nose was too large for him to be considered handsome, his black hair, peppered at the temples with sprays of gray, distinguished him, and his voice was engaging. His dark eyes, matching his olive complexion, were steady.

There was an awkward silence.

"Do you come to watch the dancers often? I, myself, come all the time," he said politely, trying to start a conversation.

"No!" Dorissa snapped, more harshly than she intended. She turned toward the dance floor as the music began. Then in a softer voice, she added, "This is my first time."

"Dance is good for the soul, don't you think?" the stranger continued, but Dorissa didn't answer. Her eyes were riveted on the musicians.

First the dumbeq player thumped out a rhythm with his fingers and palms on the goat skin of his jarlike drum. Then the oud, kanoon, and flute players joined in.

"A dancer named Aneera will be first. She usually performs on Friday evenings, I think," the stranger noted, trying to be pleasant.

"Aneera's my teacher. I study at her studio," Dorissa said proudly.

The man started to say something, but just then Aneera, with a silver-fringed and red-sequined costume wrapped in a red veil of sheer material, entered. She circled around the small dance floor a few times, clicking her cymbals and moving rapidly. Then, as the music slowed to a sensuous tempo, she began to remove the red veil that covered her.

Dorissa moved to the edge of her chair, intent on every move her teacher made. A waiter tried to interrupt her concentration. When he finally penetrated her consciousness, she quickly ordered the first appropriate item that flashed into mind: "ouzo."

Aneera, slowly removing her veil, revealed her fluttering, rolling stomach with its glittering, red-glass jewel pasted over the navel. Dorissa noticed that she wore heavy eyelashes, bright rouge, and lipstick. Her breasts were pushed up high and together by a red, sequined bra, which drooped beaded tassles from its tips. She looked hard and slick in a way she never looked in class. Going around to the men sitting at the edge of the dance floor, she shook her breasts in their faces or bumped her hips toward their shoulders. Dorissa was mesmerized by the red jewel in Aneera's navel. Her eyes moved up and down with Aneera's belly rolls.

The air was thick with smoke—the strong smell of French and Turkish tobacco. Dorissa took several gulps of Ouzo. The man across from her was now smiling at Aneera as she writhed on the floor at the feet of the musicians, who blinked not an eye as they played a chefti telli rhythm. Their authentic Middle Eastern instruments were plugged into amplifiers so that the ethnic music blared like American acid rock. Spectators talked, laughed, and drank, now and then focusing on Aneera.

As Aneera concluded, she solicited money from the male customers—a practice of the cafe dancer with which Dorissa was unfamiliar. Aneera went to each man in the audience and undulated her belly or shimmied her breasts at him until he took a dollar bill from his pocket. With a leer or an amused smile, each man tucked his money into Aneera's sequined belt or bra. Some let their fingers slip inside the garment along with the cash.

When Aneera came to Dorissa's table and shook her breasts in front of the dark-haired man, he smiled and put a dollar bill in her cleavage. Dorissa, now high on ouzo, felt a sudden fury welling within. She leaped up, snatched the money from the dancer's bosom, and threw it down on the table. Grabbing a dollar from her own purse, she pushed it into Aneera's hand.

"What's the matter?" asked the surprised Aneera, recognizing Dorissa as her student.

"This dance is a sacred ritual to the Earth Mother goddess, not a cheap burlesque," Dorissa growled to her random companion. Then, feeling the flush of embarrassment and tears of frustration stinging her face, Dorissa whirled and walked quickly out of the cafe, stopping only to pay her tab.

The dark-haired man followed Dorissa out into the street, where he found her standing on the street corner, eyes wet, looking this way and that, trying to decide which direction would take her home.

"Are you all right, miss?" he asked. "I'm sorry if I offended you. You seem very upset. Can I call you a cab?"

"No, I'm walking home. Which way is downtown?" she responded in a dull, empty voice.

"I don't think it's wise for a woman like you to walk around here alone so late at night. Can I see you to the subway? Unfortunately, I'm told I'm a perfect gentleman," he added, trying to make a joke of it.

Dorissa looked up. The man was smiling pleasantly. She sensed that he really meant to be kind. "I'm sorry. I'll be all right in a minute. The train's that way, isn't it?"

"Yes, but let me walk with you. My neighbor had an unfortunate incident, right in this area, just a week ago. I've lived in New York too many years to be overly cautious; these days everyone one knows has been mugged at least once."

"I haven't. But then I don't usually go out by myself at night." The silent atmosphere of the street seemed threatening after the heat and noise of the cafe. She was glad not to be alone on the deserted corner. They began to walk toward the subway.

"My job takes me out and around at all hours. I'm public-relations director for the Cosmopolitan Opera."

He took Dorissa's elbow as she stepped down the curb. Then he let it go. She wasn't sure whether he was being too familiar or just gentlemanly.

26

They walked a block, their shoes clicking in the midnight silence. Finally, Dorissa spoke.

"It must be interesting work—public relations for the opera."

"Not as interesting as being a dancer, I'm sure. You did say you were a dancer?"

She remembered the explanation she gave for joining him at his table. "Yes, I guess I did."

"I wanted to be a dancer for a time when I was young, but I decided to sing instead. Obviously I made the wrong choice. So I opted for PR work, instead."

She became aware of his melodious and deep voice.

"I studied ballet for a while in my early years," he went on, filling up the silence with his sonorous voice. "I wasn't bad at it, but I think my older brother intimidated me into feeling like a sissy. He was a star quarterback. By the time I was too old to care what he thought, I was also too old for the ballet—and nearly too old to be a singer."

He laughed. She began to feel safe talking to him. His manner wasn't overbearing. They'd come to the subway turnstile and the downtown train was approaching. It rumbled into the station nearly drowning out their words.

"Do you have a token?" he asked, reaching into his pocket. "I've got an extra one, here." He deposited the token for her, and she thanked him as she pushed through the turnstile and ran for the train. "You know it's absolutely true what you said about the belly dance being an ancient fertility ritual!" he shouted after her as she ran ahead.

She leaped onto the train, and the doors closed behind her. She was sorry to have left him so abruptly. She would have liked to talk with him longer, but didn't want to seem to stall for a pickup. She sat down and absentmindedly looked at the subway posters. One, sponsored by The National Organization for Women bore the statistics of women dead from illegal abortions from 1941 to the present. Remembering her own close call with such a death, she shuddered.

As she exited the train station at Sheridan Square, she looked up to notice that the fellow bowing aside for her to pass through the turnstile was the deep-voiced stranger from the cafe.

"I guess we get off at the same stop!" he said, not wanting her to think his presence deliberate.

"I didn't see you get on the train," she answered, puzzling.

"I ran for another car, I guess. I live on Waverly Place, near here."

She was glad to see him again. She thought she never would.

"I'm on West Fourth. My name's Dorissa Femfunelli."

"A melodious Italian name. I thought you looked rather like a Botticelli—maybe one of the Three Dancing Graces!"

They reached the top of the subway stairwell and paused awhile in the street. "Where do you dance? Maybe I can come and watch you sometime?"

To avoid answering, Dorissa paused to buy a copy of *Majority Voice* at the corner newsstand.

"May I be so presumptuous as to ask why you were so upset at the cafe? I know it's none of my business, but . . ."

"I think it's an ugly custom—tipping that way."

"You're obviously not a *belly* dancer."

"Well, here's my building. Thanks for walking me. I appreciate it."

"I wish we could talk a little longer. But I don't suppose you'd invite an old man like me for coffee, would you? As I said, I'm told I'm a perfect gentleman."

Noah Levi-Museman was, indeed, a gentleman. He sat on the floor talking with Dorissa, under the sparse branches of her Avocado Tree, until 3:23 A.M. and never laid a hand on her breasts, buttocks, or knees. When she finally showed him to the door, he simply kissed her hand, bowing a little in the European style.

Dorissa laid awake until 4:36 A.M. thinking of all the facts, implications, and dreams they'd conveyed to one another. She discovered that he was actually fifty-five years old—something he rarely admitted to anyone. At one point in the evening, during their discussion of ethnic dances, he had jumped up to demonstrate a few difficult Cossack leaps. As he took off his jacket and loosened his tie, she noticed that his arms were muscular and his neck strong and sinewy.

"I'm a great believer in exercise," he explained. "I work out at the gym whenever I can. Calisthenics. Those ballet lessons gave me a good, healthy foundation. If you have it when you're young and work just a little at it, you never lose it. Any strenuous exercise like tennis, jogging, dancing, or work that works up a sweat is good for the psyche, too. It produces more neuro-adrenaline, and neuro-adrenaline is an antidepressant hormone. You were so right to take up dancing when you found yourself in a fit of depression. Your natural instinct was perfect."

"You have a rational explanation for everything!" laughed Dorissa. "You're incredible." She felt comfortable with Noah. He was so fatherly and empathetic that she explained Oliver's insults and her artistic disillusionment at the cafe.

"No wonder you were upset. My tipping Aneera in her bosom reminded you of Oliver's insults." Noah understood perfectly. "I'm afraid we men are all alike. I myself am a rather foolish one, attracted to a beautiful woman like yourself. But not enough of a Don Juan." He confessed that a young woman he had met at a fund-raising party for the opera stood him up at the cafe that evening. Then he told Dorissa that he was married to a woman who had been in a mental institution for the past six years.

"She was a lovely poet, but just too sensitive for this world. Now that I look back, I realize that it was her instability, her incredible insight and wild imagination that attracted me. She finally lost her grip on reality. It's very sad. My daughters are grown and well, thank heaven. They're going to school in England. It takes every extra cent I have to send them to school there, but it's good for them to be far away from their mother's illness. When I visit her, she just stares through me as if I were the ghost of someone she's never known. I talk to the doctors and nurses. Last time, when I brought her flowers, she just took them in her lap and looked at them for a long time. Then she picked a rose from the bunch and slowly counted the petals, tearing them one by one from their stem. She gave me the empty stalk, and I went home with it. . . . That's all. . . . It's hard to believe now that we were ever so close, discussed everything, had children, brought them up together. . . .

"I know I shouldn't say this, but you remind me of her a little —all the nice things that made me fall in love with her when we were young. You're as beautiful as she was then, even more so. . . ."

A week later, as they sat in his brownstone apartment—cluttered with books, *Playbills*, copies of *Opera News*, and shabby antiques—Dorissa teased Noah: "You don't have to give me nice compliments to get me to do the dishes!"

He sat beside her on a faded sofa. As she talked, he listened attentively. "I read that primitive women give birth in a kneeling or squatting position, instinctively pushing the baby out with their belly muscles. I wish I could have given birth to Chrysta that way. Squatting down on the earth. Ecstatic with pain. My legs on the ground. I'm sure that's where the floorwork part of the belly dance comes from. It's a birth mime."

Noah took her hand and held it. She liked the warm reassurance of his touch. She leaned against his shoulder. Then he kissed her on the lips. For a long time, they stood holding each other and feeling the warmth of their bodies. They were both hesitant.

Finally, Dorissa took him by the hand and led him into the bedroom. He opened her blouse. The lights filtering in from the living room made her pale flesh glow in the darkness. She was aware of the hunger he felt—the chemistry that drew him to her. Suddenly his hands were all over her, feeling her breasts. Then he stepped back, as if embarrassed.

She moved to the bed, sitting down on a pile of paperback books. She felt a weakness in her knees and a wetness between her legs. She hadn't made love to anyone in months except for the mistaken night with Oliver. She ached a little with desire. The faint pain in her groin made her feel vulnerable. She wanted to cry.

He came to her and stood over her and took her face in his hands. "I'm twenty-two years older than you," he said quietly. He felt shy. "The only women I've slept with in a long time are these books."

"You're just you," she answered, pressing the side of her face to his stomach. His belt was hard and cold against her cheek. She boldly unbuckled it and opened the waist button of his pants.

Slowly, they helped each other undress. She felt the tremendous need his hands communicated. It was as if being wanted was the best aphrodisiac. He pushed himself into her and moved a little inside of her. She was thrilled by the sensations of his movements. But then he drew himself out and asked if she was protected. She felt foolish, like a silly girl too stupid to take care of herself.

"Never mind. It's all right," he assured her.

Anxious to satisfy him, she took his penis in her mouth, as she'd once done with Oliver. He was so thoroughly excited that in a moment he released himself with a primal groan. She tasted him, filling her mouth in spurts and held her lips firmly around him until the spasms ceased. They rested for a while. Noah lay on his back, holding her in his arms. With his hand, he discovered how moist she was. He touched her, then moved down to press his lips between her legs and flick his tongue against her clitoris. Her wetness pleased him, but she was too self-conscious of her female body and its aroma to relax completely.

She pulled him upward. "Lie next to me and hold me. Touch me with your hand," she whispered.

Never before had she had the courage to ask directly for the stimulation of her own pleasure. She'd thought that Oliver could sense intuitively from her squirms and moans what she wanted and so never asked for more than he gave. But with Noah, she felt so secure, she wasted no time playing a moaning woman's symphony of longing.

After several frustrating months of married love that had brought her almost, but not quite, to the highest pitch of ecstasy, she'd discovered masturbation, an activity repressed and conditioned out of her by her upbringing. Later, when she was finally able to experience orgasm with Oliver, it was too late for sexual ecstasy to coincide with love. Sex got better as love got worse, and finally anger destroyed both.

Enough femininity had encountered Noah's sensitivity to make him deeply desirous of fulfilling her. He moved his hand eagerly and patiently, feeling more and more excited as her excitement increased. Finally he heard her cry of ecstasy. It was as if demons were released from her in a sexual exorcism.

STEP 4:

The Stomach Flutter

"You've quit!" Oliver screamed. "Are you crazy?"

Dorissa held the phone away from her ear.

"I haven't quit, Oliver. I've just taken a leave of absence to develop my dancing career!"

"What dancing career? How are you going to support yourself? What about Chrysta? Have you gone completely mad?"

"I can't talk to you now," Dorissa answered. "I have an appointment with my agent."

"Your agent?"

Before Oliver could continue, Dorissa hung up the phone. She didn't care what Oliver thought. If he didn't understand, fatherly Noah did, but Oliver's question, "What about Chrysta?" troubled her. The little girl had come to live with her in her tiny Greenwich Village apartment.

On her daughter's first night there, Dorissa tiptoed across the floor of the child's bedroom and stood looking down at Chrysta's face in its calm repose. Her child lived, umbilicus cut, a separate being from herself, a unique individual with thoughts, desires, dreams, longings, memories all her own. People had always told her that Chrysta looked like her. Dorissa was aware of the resemblance, but it was as if she were seeing it, herself, for the first time. The child's face was smaller, younger, more childlike, but Dorissa had the profound sense of looking down at herself as if she were looking into a clear pool of water. It startled her. There were the same wide-set eyes with their dark brown lashes, the same pale northern Italian complexion, the same high cheekbones and square-boned chin, the same closely set, even, white teeth, the same long earlobes, pug nose, and heart-shaped lips, the same auburn-blond hair, with its tendency to get too curly whenever it rained.

Dorissa winced at the thought of her own disillusioning initiations into womanhood and remembering her own pubertal traumas, she felt an overwhelming tenderness for the innocent child who slept so peacefully. She wondered what would become of this life she'd had the vanity to procreate.

She had only meant to take the next day off when she'd left St. Aloysius the afternoon before, but she found herself saying, "I'm not coming back tomorrow, or any other day!" The principal told her she was upset and hysterical over her divorce and should take a leave of absence to recuperate. He had patted her hand like a benevolent father.

Whatever it was called, Dorissa was collecting unemployment. Noah had secured the names of a few talent agencies that handled variety acts. She'd phoned around until she found one that was willing to give her an interview. The agency was located on West Forty-seventh Street near "The Great White Way."

Dorissa climbed a dimly lit staircase and took an elevator to the thirteenth floor. The hallway was lined with frosted glass doors painted with black letters spelling out the names of small firms. Finally, she found the one: "As You-Like-It, Variety Acts, Inc." A Clairol redhead sat just inside the door, painting her fingernails with a dark blue polish. The acrid polish assaulted Dorissa's nostrils. "I'm here to see Pat Campley," she announced with feigned confidence.

"Your name?" asked the receptionist.

"Dorissa Femfunelli."

"Dorissa . . . ?"

"*Femfunelli.*"

"Dorissa Femfunjelly to see you," said the redhead, being careful not to mess her wet nailpolish on the button of the intercom. She took a copy of *Mademoiselle* and of *Vogue* out of her desk. "Right through that door, Miss Femfunjelly."

Dorissa opened the door to the inner office and spied a large, gray-blond, squarely built man with a white boutonniere in his blue lapel. He sat behind a big mahogany desk from the vaudeville era. The whole office seemed like something out of *Ziegfeld's Follies.*

"Come in, dear," said the large, gray-blond man in a light and airy voice, very precise in diction. "Sit down and we'll talk first."

Dorissa seated herself and there was a long pause. She didn't know exactly how to begin. Just as she was about to speak, the man asked impatiently:

"Well, where are your pictures and résumé? Your publicity clippings and such?"

"I . . . I don't have any . . . not yet . . . I mean . . ." Dorissa muttered, trying to be cheerful about it.

"Oh well, my dear, that's too bad. How old are you?"

"Thirty-three." She wasn't sure of the importance of his question.

"Thirty-three and no résumé! Tsk, tsk, tsk. What do ya do, sing?"

"I'm a dancer."

"A dancer? Thirty-three and without a résumé? What kind of a dancer?"

"A . . . birth dancer—that is, a belly dancer, but really a *birth* dancer," said Dorissa, haltingly.

"A birth dancer, huh, kid?" Pat Campley began leafing through a pile of papers on his desk. "What's a birth dancer, sweetie? I don't get it." He pushed back the chair and lit a cigarette, carefully placed in a white ivory holder. He looked at her knees, her hands, her breasts, and at last, into her eyes. She noted the faded blue color of his. "What did you say your name was?"

Nervously, Dorissa launched into an explanation of her research of the belly dance as an ancient childbirth preparation. Pat Campley regarded her coldly. She found she couldn't quite bring herself to go into it as a boon to the elimination of menstrual cramps. She'd assumed from her telephone conversation that Pat Campley, with his high-pitched voice, was a female. It was disappointing not to be able to appeal to his womanhood with her scheme, but she proceeded as best she could.

The square-boned talent agent watched her intently as she rambled, telling of her desire to "birth dance" for women's groups, rotary clubs, church bazaars, and feminist organizations like NOW. She wanted to excite women about natural childbirth and the healthy freedom of their bodies. Her talk became more inspired than she realized.

When she finished, dubbing her routine "The new dance of liberation for today's sexually free female," Pat Campley began to laugh, then giggle. Finally he leaned forward, smiling, and patted her on the knee, as if he were her schoolchum. "Let's see you do your stuff. The audition room's in there." He indicated a door behind him.

Dorissa felt like slapping his wrist and telling him to fuck off, but she decided if she had gotten this far with her first agent, she might as well continue. Picking up her costume and canvas bag, she asked: "Where do I change?"

"Oh well, if you want privacy, I'll wait out here in the office. I just love costumes, dearie. Hope you brought a pretty one." Mr. Campley giggled.

Dorissa entered the dingy audition room. A small stage with old-fashioned footlights stood at the far side. Two rows of very dim globes hung from the ceiling, casting shadows over antique wooden theater chairs with worn red mohair upholstery. Afraid that Pat Campley would enter before she could finish, she changed quickly.

Many hours of work had gone into the costume she donned. She'd made it herself, carefully sewing amber and green beads over a halter-type bra covered with fern green satin. Her flared, avocado green, chiffon skirt was worn, in the usual belly dancer's style, a few inches below the navel. It was adorned by a seven-pound, trinketed, and beaded belt. She jingled it with shimmies to be sure it was securely in place. She'd learned that belly dancers wear heavy hip belts in order to feel their hips wiggle. Finally, she wrapped an expanse of sheer veiling, with a tie-died, leafy pattern, around her face and body.

She took a deep breath. "Ready, Mr. Campley!" she called.

Campley sauntered in with a brandy snifter in one hand and sat down. "I'll turn on the lights for you, honey. So I can really see you do your belly." He giggled softly. "Okay, dear, let me have it." The footlights blazed up at the stage as Dorissa turned on her tape recorder.

She could hear her musical cues, but it was as if she wasn't there. She went blindly through the routine she'd rehearsed many times with Noah for an attentive audience. He'd given her artistic pointers, until, between the two of them, she'd choreographed a belly-rolling ritual, suggestive of an ancient Egyptian morisco. In bed with her one night, he'd read from his handy paperback copy of *The Dance of Life* by Havelock Ellis.

"Humanity's most primitive impulse is toward the dance as an expression of the flux and flow of the universe," Noah had declared, kissing her passionately. "The season of love is a time that the nubile of each sex devote to dancing in an effort to display the force, energy, skill, endurance, beauty, and grace that yearn within them to be poured into the stream of life!"

After they'd made ardent love in his rumpled, book-littered bed, Dorissa danced, rolling naked on Noah's parquet floors, as if deeply involved in pagan Earth worship. Her consistent research documented her birth dance of Earth. Depicted throughout history, on African cave walls, Thebian tombs, Greek burial vases, Roman frescoes of Bacchanalian rites, Etruscan bas-reliefs, and Persian temples, she discovered pictures of women dancing homage to ancient goddesses.

Blooming with the aura of sexual love inspired by flashes of Noah's intellect, Dorissa had come to feel like a primitive priestess of Isis or Diana.

Now dancing for Pat Campley, she removed her veil very slowly. Then as the rhythm changed to a sensuous Greek and Arabic chefti telli, she threw her veil aside and went into a birth mime, twisting and writing on the floor, kneeling, leaning back, rolling her stomach. She executed an enticing step called the Stomach Flutter, which blended impressively with the butterflies in her stomach.

Hold your breath in your throat and pant the belly rapidly in and out like an overheated puppy. The stomach should flutter in small, quick movements.

She rose from the floor and danced around the stage as if celebrating an orgiastic climax.

Finally, she swept into a final bow as Campley giggled: "Charming. Nice. Very sensual. I like it. It's an adorable idea."

"You mean you'll represent me? You see," she said animatedly, "I'd lecture to the women first—explain the history, primitive obstetrics, and all that! It's good for menstrual cramps, too. . . ." The dancing had freed her inhibitions. She felt invigorated and burst forth with a new torrent of explanations.

"Wait a minute, sweetheart," interrupted Campley. "Don't get all excited. I don't get too many calls from women's rotary clubs and church groups for *belly* dancers! We'll have to advertise. It's very special—unless you want to try the cafe scene?"

"Oh I see," Dorissa said, coming down from the high created by her dancing.

"You're so luscious. We'll find a way to promote you. We'll have to package you in a dignified way and still sell the belly dance. It won't be easy. Can you afford to invest in a few publicity pics and brochures?"

"Afford to invest *money?*" Dorissa asked, unsure of his meaning.

"Yes, *money!* You silly little thing! What did you think I meant?" he giggled. "I'm not that sort of fellow. Think of me as one of your *girl*friends. I'm not a fag and I do like women, but I never take advantage of my position. So don't worry, honey, you can relax. This *is* New York, but there are still a few decent people left. How are you fixed for money?"

"Well, I don't have any. Maybe I can save some and come back again," she added sadly.

"Well, we can't let the agency put out the bread for something

37

so risky—not until we see if we can get rotary clubs and feminist groups to go for your kind of number. We could start a little branch agency, to capitalize on the movement, call it "Women's Lib Talent, Inc.," or something—just another letterhead to drum up trade. Do you belong to AGVA?"

"AGVA?"

"Association of Guild and Variety Artists! What else, baby doll? We'll have to change your name. Dorissa Femfingellilly will never do."

"My father will be furious. Do we have to?"

"Of course, but we can't even get started until we get some capital together. We really only need a few hundred to get started. You've got music and a costume. Where did you get it? I haven't seen anything like that at Bloomingdale's."

"I made it myself!" Dorissa answered, proud of the seamstress abilities her mother, Sophia, had bestowed on her. She was annoyed with Pat Campley's fast talk, but she was determined to listen to what he had to say. He seemed to have the *business* sense she lacked about the whole thing.

"Clever girl! You're resourceful—which gives me an idea!" He fingered some beads on her belt, admiring Dorissa's handywork. "Get dressed and come back into my office. I want to check my files."

As Dorissa sat at his deskside, he explained: "We've got a list of Christmas parties and such coming up for the holidays. You'll make a few hundred bucks to spend on brochures and mailings. Here's one, right here, for Christmas Eve. Brand & Brand, Inc., a frozen fast-foods firm in New Jersey, just the other side of the Lincoln Tunnel, in the suburbs off Route 3. You'll pick up a couple hundred in one night. We can start taking pictures for your brochures as soon as you get your check." He flipped his file box shut and handed her a card with an address.

She was hesitant to perform before an audience, but, thrilled that Pat Campley didn't think her idea too outlandish to work, she took the address card in her hand. The fact that he was willing to help her launch her little venture gave her hope that she might actually establish a dance career. She would enjoy nothing better than forcing Oliver to apologize for his insults.

STEP 5:

The Stomach Flutter Repeated

On Christmas Eve at three in the morning, her first dance performance fatefully finished, Dorissa entered the dark solitude of her Greenwich Village apartment. She flopped down in a rumpled heap beneath her Avocado Tree. She'd given up spending Christmas Eve with Chrysta in order to dance at the Brand & Brand party. The evening's fiasco conglomerated in painful images in her limp, lugubrious mind: The white middle-class couples sipping iced alcoholic drinks, served by black maids, had seemed deceptively sedate at first. She'd planned to deliver a brief lecture on her ancient woman's ritual, but by the time she performed, after midnight, it was difficult to subdue the uproariously drunken bunch.

"Oh come on, honey, take it off!" shouted one male heckler. "The belly dance is a sexy slave dance. We don't want none of your women's lib shit. This is a *drinking* party!"

Hopelessly, Dorissa tried to explain that the belly dance became a harem treat only after the fall of matriarchal civilization. "Just as the American Indian has come to dance his sacred rituals to attract tourist trade to the reservation, so woman has come to perform her birth dance in the cafes of modern cities all over the world!" she shouted, momentarily undaunted.

"Cut the bullshit, baby, and show us your stuff!" laughed the heckler, who received a jab in the stomach from his mortified wife.

Her audience tipped their glasses, lit cigarettes, and waited for what they had been promised, a belly dancer.

She gave up, flipped her switch, and began numbly to dance, slowly removing her veil, only to be greeted by catcalls. Amid the din of laughter and joking, she felt like a comic burlesque queen. Finally she tried to get some of the women present to join her in the celebratory climax of her dance, but, embarrassed, they giggled and insisted they couldn't. At last, one woman got up and began to wiggle her ample, miniskirted bottom.

"That a girl, Joannie! Show us your stuff!" the heckler laughed. "I'll get you up against the water cooler on Monday!"

Dorissa felt thoroughly discouraged by her attempt to celebrate the Earth Mother in New Jersey on Christmas Eve. When the president of Brand & Brand barged in on her while she was changing, it was the last straw. She pushed the drunken, breast-'n'-buttock-grabbing fellow into the Deluxe Whirlpool, sunken bathtub of his fully gadgeted, Christmas-lamp-lit, suburban home.

Now, in just a few hours, she'd have to face Christmas Day at her mother-in-law's with Oliver, and watch him frown as Chrysta opened up her presents. Oliver always left all the shopping to Dorissa and then complained about what she bought. Chrysta would unwrap a book from Noah—A Child's ABC of Organic, Vegetarian Eating, a pair of Syrian finger cymbals, a red-stretch leotard, and a six-week gift certificate for lessons in the mother/daughter belly dancing class at Aneera's studio.

"Are you out of your head? You want to make your daughter into a go-go dancer, too?" Oliver would say, disapprovingly. Then she'd have to try to explain patiently that Chrysta, now eight, came to class with her to observe, and the child begged to have lessons. She'd have to tell him that in the Middle East, daughters are taught to dance, from a very early age, by their mothers, that it is a therapy dance for women passed on from generation to generation. Oliver would continue to disapprove. The rest of the day would be spent in relative discomfort, smiling at her in-laws and avoiding Oliver's gaze.

A huge internal sob emanated from her psyche and floated in silent waves up the trunk of the Avocado Tree, which dolefully leaned its eye-shaped leaves down over her.

Quite literally feeling her sadness, the Tree spoke in a subliminal voice. It reached her mind, bypassing her eardrums, sending waves of biophysical energy directly into her brain. When its thought patterns reassembled in her mind they possessed a tone as melodious as Billie Burke's playing the Good Witch of the North in Hollywood's *Wizard of Oz*.

"Don't give up, dear," said the Avocado Tree. "Remember, Isadora said that the dancer of the future would dance the freedom of women . . . the highest intelligence in the freest body!"

Dorissa, inexplicably feeling a little bit better, finally fell asleep. Visions of the suburban kitchen she'd waited in earlier that evening, before her performance, danced in her head. Along Formica counters stood toasters, rotisseries, automatic juice-extractors, electric coffee grinders, electric frypans, mixers, blenders, ossifiers, automatic can-openers, meat slicers, garbage disposals, dishwashers, and sundry other gadgets, all ignored by black caterers who unwrapped preprocessed foods transported in plastic wrappers to the premises. A dreamy vision of the president of Brand & Brand lying in his sunken, Whirlpool bathtub, cursing and blubbering, was interrupted by the sounding of the telephone. For a brief bewildered moment, Dorissa didn't know where she was. She reached out from under her warm blanket and picked up the receiver. "Hello," she said in a sleepy, anxious voice. The thought that something might be wrong with Chrysta flashed through her subconscious.

"Listen to me," answered a strange male voice. "I have your place staked out, and if you don't let me make love to you on the telephone, I'm going to come over there and take care of you. I'm going to rip off your nightgown and fuck your cunt till it's sore."

41

Dorissa was suddenly awake and thinking quickly. First of all, she wasn't wearing a nightgown, and second, the man had only threatened to "fuck" her if she didn't let him make "love" to her on the telephone. It wasn't the first obscene call she'd received during the course of her life in New York City.

She spoke directly into the receiver in a sympathetic tone: "You listen to me! You're sick, and you need help. Having to resort to calling up strange women in the middle of the night is sad. I feel sorry for you. Obviously, your parents or someone did something awful to you when you were little and made you sick about sex. You need to find a healthy outlet. Believe me. It took a long time for me to sort it all out for myself. You don't need to resort to being a telephone rapist. I really feel sorry for you. You should get help!"

When she finished her sincere speech, there was nothing but silence at the other end of the wire umbilicus that reached out to some strange man in the litter of humanity huddled at the edge of the Atlantic Ocean—the biggest city in the most affluent and technologically advanced civilization the world had ever known. There was a pause of silence, and Dorissa said: "Are you still there?"

The man's sigh entered her ear. "Where can I get help?" he uttered in a pitiful voice, bereft of its threatening tone. But before she could tell him that she herself didn't know, there was a click and the receiver went dead, leaving its vacuum of anonymity against her ear.

———◆———

Before the receptionist could stop her, Ms. Femfunelli, adrenaline coursing through her, barged into Pat Campley's office the morning after Christmas. She had an uncomfortable suspicion that her obscene caller had been the chief executive of Brand & Brand, Inc., and had no intention of dancing at any more parties. She'd resolved to take her hard-earned money and go. Her anger turned to bewilderment as she found Mr. Campley standing in front of a mirror dressed in a belly dancing costume that looked

42

rented from Minsky's, all sequins, fringes, and tassels, false breasts, and gold lamé.

"Oh dear, you weren't announced!" he chortled anxiously. "Oh well, I'm just trying to figure out how you do that trick with your tummy—when you flutter it real fast. It's so *sexy*," said Pat Campley, as if there were nothing unusual in his appearance.

Dorissa turned to go, feeling she'd walked in on something quite private, but her violent curiosity detained her. Her jaw dropped, and she stared in amazement at the peculiar belly dancer. Mr. Campley felt obliged to offer an explanation.

"You've gone and caught me, dearie. Now you'll have to listen to my spiel. You females aren't the only oppressed gender!" he declared, whipping a paperback book from his desk drawer as a cowboy whips out a pistol, or a mystery detective a gun.

"Read this!" he demanded, thrusting the paperback into Dorissa's hands. She read the title: *Understanding the Transvestite*. "We TVs have to get our rights, too!" he insisted, wiggling his fringes and jiggling his beads.

He wanted to help her, he confessed, because he was really quite "turned on" by her dancing and wanted to dance like her. He envied her woman's body and suffered clitoris envy as surely as any woman ever suffered Freudian penis envy. He was a man hung up on the image of the Hollywood sex kitten, envious of the silver-screen fate of a Harlow or a Monroe. He was erotically aroused by wearing women's clothes because he really wanted to change his entire identity to female. He desired the love of a woman as well. He dreamed of being Joan Crawford, in pink pantyhose, making love to Barbara Stanwyck, in purple pantyhose. He longed to grow breasts, shave his legs, invert his penis, and be treated like a sex object.

Dorissa stood fascinated as Pat Campley poignantly expounded his estrogen envy. She had never before been confronted with the phenomenon of tranvestism. Here she was trying to get free of her sexual stereotype, while this man ached to embody it. Some quirk of his fatherless childhood had cultivated, in Pat Campley, a travesty of female vanity, a longing for mincing femininity.

The poor fellow explained that it was terribly hard for him to find another human being to fulfill his fantasy, so he had to resort

43

to auto-eroticism. He opened up a locked cabinet and revealed his poignant loneliness to Dorissa. An army of pink, blue, and white plastic vibrators invaded her eyes. She sat dumfounded as he showed her the various "pros" and "cons" of each model, pointing out the advantages of this or that feature or attachment.

He finished his tale of woe and noticed that Dorissa stood dazed. "What's the matter? Are you shocked, honey?" he queried, going to her and putting his arm supportively around her shoulder as he wiped a tear from the corner of his eye with a pink Kleenex. "No," she answered dully. "I'm emotionally exhausted." She collapsed into a chair. She felt empathy for Campley. He was one more wounded duck limping through the skies of sexual repression and psychological quirk. If she had had trouble finding ordinary, heterosexual love, how much more difficult for him to find love at all. Even obscene phone callers made her feel more sad than angry, but if people were so sick and messed up, how was she ever going to dance her sensual erotic liberty for them? Where would she find people who didn't need to giggle or leer at a woman's body or make "dirty" jokes?

Pat Campley in his garish gold lamé, sequined, and fringed costume made her feel more hopeless.

"*Madre mia*," she aspirated inadvertently.

"Oh call me that again," blurted Pat Campley. "It really turns me on! Couldn't you just throw me down, right now, on the desk and rape me? Just once? I'd love it."

In answer, Dorissa slumped lower in her chair and started to weep.

"Oh sweetie, I didn't mean to upset you! Wait. I'll change back into my street clothes and then you'll feel better," said Pat Campley with genuine concern.

"It's not your clothes. It's all the twisted sex and upset mess of everything. I don't know what to do!" Dorissa continued, distraught. "Last night was a disaster!"

"Didn't they like your dancing? I think you're sexier than Theda Bara," assured Mr. Campley, adjusting his false bosoms.

"You don't understand any better than they did!" moaned Dorissa. "The men treated me like a go-go dancer or a burlesque queen, and the women were just bewildered. I guess I was crazy to

44

come here in the first place. I'll end up teaching watered-down so-cial studies to disturbed teen-agers for the rest of my life! That's exactly what Oliver wants me to do." Dorissa reached for a pink Kleenex from the silver cardboard dispenser on the desk.

"Who's Oliver?"

"Oliver's my *former* husband!" She blew her nose. "I became a teacher because it was a respectable profession for a professor's wife and I got married, like a good Italian girl, because I lost my virginity. Teaching wouldn't be so bad if you could really tell the truth to sick sophomores whose parents mess them up. There's no way they would understand you."

"Well, they'd certainly have trouble understanding me!" He sat down and crossed his legs. One hairy panty-hosed limb showed it-self, prominently thrust through the slit in his gold lamé skirt. "What did you say to the obscene caller? Gee, I wish I'd get one. I'd love it . . . but not from a *man*, on second thought."

"I told him he was sick and that he needed help," she an-swered, matter-of-factly.

"What a little Jewish mother you are, honey!" He laughed, wig-gling his fringes.

"What an ecological disaster you are, baby." She returned the laugh. "You have more junk on than my trash can. What kind of taste did your mother have? She was obviously a combination of Carmen Miranda and Sophie Tucker!"

They both laughed. They'd established a rapport.

She began to launch into her lecture about the birth dance of Earth again, but Pat Campley stopped her.

"Look, honey. This time I'm going to level with you! I'm so turned on by you, I really want to help you. I'd love to worship at the shrine of your Earth Mother's pubis! I understand exactly what you're saying. You can be *my* high priestess any time, but most people aren't capable of sublime thoughts about femi-nine humanism. They aren't going to see anything but sex in what you're doing. You'll just have to put your ass on the line and settle for being plain *sexy!*"

"It's not my ass I want to put on the line. It's my belly." She became a little furious with him.

"Then see if you can roll your belly on CBS and NBC *The me-*

45

dium is the message. That's where the mentality of this country is at!"

"You're right," she sighed sadly, grabbing another pink tissue. "Morroe Berger says that vindicating the belly dance in America would require a cultural conversion of the entire civilization!"

"Who is Morroe Berger? You're losing me again, sweets!"

"A Princeton scholar who wrote about the origins of the belly dance." She remembered Noah's teaching.

"Will you come off it with the Princeton scholars, already? This is show biz, baby. Show *biz!* But don't be depressed. You've earned a little toward your publicity campaign. We may still be able to make the whole thing click the way you want it to." Pat Campley uncrossed his legs and leaned forward to check the Rolodex file on his desk. "Let me see. I think I can get you a job where you'll really be able to do your thing."

Dorissa was too disheartened, "No thanks, Mr. Campley. I'll just take my money and go, if you don't mind. I guess I'd better go back to St. Aloysius. Meantime, I'll make an appointment with the unemployment office."

"Whatever you say, dearie. Go home and put your feet up and relax. We'll talk about it in a few weeks. You really need to take these setbacks in your stride. Making it as a belly dancing priestess of feminism isn't going to be easy!"

Before Dorissa could leave in the state of renewed depression that now replaced her rage, he added, "Honey, please do me a big favor and teach me how to do that trick with your tummy."

Hold your breath and pant with your stomach muscles so that your belly moves quickly in and out, as if it were a duck's gullet gulping down food. This breathless pant of the belly muscles is easier than it looks. Later, the Stomach Flutter can be combined with the Hip Circle or the Belly Roll for a doubly exciting effect.

STEP 6:

The Shoulder Shake

Dorissa knew, though Pat Campley was an unusual person, that he had hit the nail on the thumb. Changing the image of the belly dance wasn't going to be easy for her. Its devolution from a sacred ritual to a cafe spectacle was probably quite irreversible. Ever since *Little Egypt* had rolled her exotic belly at the Chicago world's fair in Victorian 1893, the ancient dance had been associated in the American mind with the burlesque hootchy-kootchy. Dorissa made the mistake of thinking that sexual attitudes had truly changed in America.

One morning, while Chrysta was at school, Dorissa, deep in a maze of depression, on the way home from the unemployment office, had accidently ridden a subway train all the way past downtown Manhattan, to Brooklyn. She had stood on a subway platform that rose above ground over the Gowanus Canal. Numbly, she peered at the people standing around her on the chilly platform in industrial South Brooklyn.

She imagined herself standing in a loincloth, unself-consciously bare-breasted, loitering alongside sun-skinned natives in the shade of a leafy green jungle. The bright contrast of color in her mind slowly faded into the bleak reality of the subway platform, with its gray concrete-and-steel surfaces. Then she saw Her. The Great Goddess, big and full, stood against the barren sky. The Statue of Liberty, like a foolishly idealistic woman, held her torch of freedom aloft on the horizon over the polluted seascape.

Spread out before the colossal, voluptuous mother of the harbor, railroad tracks carried trains, highways roared with trucks, and erect factory stacks ejaculated smoke into a thick yellowish-gray air unfit for human consumption. Absolutely nowhere was there a tree or a shrub to be seen. Not a speck of green vegetation dotted the land. The noisy, coughing, and grumbling industrial basin spread out beyond the train ramp, a barren sculpture chipped out of rock and steel by the chisel of greed.

Dorissa Femfunelli saw the smoke rising from its stacks and factory chimneys and thought how her parents had worked their way, steerage passage, to the New World, waiting anxiously, herded on the deck of their crowded ship, to catch a glimpse of Liberty's light. She imagined all the pop-top cans, bottles, boxes, jars, and plastic wrappers being manufactured in the geometric brick-and-concrete structures erected beneath the womanly figure. It was the strangest view of the familiar statue that Dorissa had ever seen. Its ghostly green hue was inviting against the pale sky. Dorissa thought of the poem by Emma Lazarus inscribed in its base. She imagined the huge green woman putting down her heavy book and torch to lift her skirts and dance. She saw her colossal hips bumping, her breasts shimmying, her giant belly rolling, her toes tripping from rooftop to rooftop. Dorissa ached to dance with her vision.

Suddenly she stepped forward to the edge of the platform, almost falling onto the tracks below, as the train screeched into the station, wiping away the view, with its graffitied expanse and rattling windows. Dazed, she boarded the train, sat down in the graffitied car amid the weary passengers, who appeared shabby in the cold, fluorescent light. The sound of coins rattling in a cup filled her ears as the train lurched and ground onward. A blind old woman made her eyeless way past the commuters. Blank faces remained fixed on newsprint. Some heads tilted on the axis of their necks, eyes closed. A few looked up at the tattered beggar and dropped coins in her cup as if to thank her for reminding them that they, at least, had sight. Seated in the swaying, screeching, stuffy car, Dorissa deposited some coins in the woman's cup and felt guilty about her own unhappiness.

Then, as the morning sanitation workers banged and rattled cans and roared their truck along West Fourth Street, she dragged herself toward home. A huge garbage truck like a dinosaur crept on rubber, automotive feet along asphalt, and accepted another load of waste into the pit of its stomach, through its grinding jaws. A litany of garbage began to play like a record beneath the groaning needle of her mind.

Tissues, tinfoil, cardboard boxes marked with the names of trendy detergents; crusts of refined white bread stuck with hydrogenated peanut butter and strained jelly; broken Coke bottles, empty beer cans, discarded containers from Librium, Valium, Miltown, aspirin, Bromo-Selzter, Alka-Seltzer, deodorants; cigarette butts, newspapers, crusted cans, and catsup-soaked wax paper brayed a litany in her brain as she entered the front door of her building.

Soggy milk containers, gooey contraceptives, bloodied Kotex, shitty disposable diapers, fat cut from steaks, dirty Band-Aids, bent clothes hangers, broken rubber bands, rusty screws, rolled toothpaste tubes, vacant lipstick dispensers; torn love letters, bank statements, crushed styrofoam; shattered glass, coffee grinds, soggy tea bags; pornographic horror comics, old *Showbills*, dead mice, mashed cockroaches; cat litter, dog dung, and aluminum foil congealed in a cacophonous litany in her cranium as she turned the key in her door.

Finally, she sank dolefully down under her Avocado Tree. Its leafy branches stirred in the breeze from the slightly opened window. The slanting winter light filtered down from the window, glazing the edges of each green, rippled leaf. She noticed the intricate system of veins woven in symmetrical patterns through their surfaces, observing the serene plants with an unbearable envy for their pristine peace, their superhuman silence. She thought of how her youth was passing. The dream prince promised in little girls' fairy tales had not arrived to whisk her away on his white charger to a castle of dreams.

"Don't despair, my dear. *The Earth Mother will have her Second Coming.* You're called as her prophet," said the Avocado Tree, via Dorissa's psychic plasma, as she fell into a brief sleep.

When she rose from her pillows and shook out her hair, she remembered an ad she'd seen advertised on the back of *Majority Voice.*

"Release your frustrations through auto-erotic revelations and feminist consciousness-raising techniques. Come to Narcissa Tittel's Body-consciousness-expanding Workshop. Call in advance for an appointment," declared the advertisement.

She telephoned Noah's office, left a message with his secretary, and then called Narcissa Tittel's automatic answering device and made a reservation for the evening workshop advertised in the paper. At first, Noah Levi-Museman had responded as Oliver Kelly had—bringing her roses and literally kissing her feet. Now that they had known each other for several months and the first deep blushes of romance had burped and farted themselves sallow, she no longer felt satisfied to wait for his calls. Pale-cheeked, she decided to stand him up for some body-consciousness expanding.

"Anything will be better than waiting with my legs in the air like a coat rack for Noah to hang his hat on—especially since he's always so wrapped up in his work that he shows up at least twenty minutes late these days," she thought.

She had spent long hours reading philosophical paperback books he had given her and dreaming of spiritual glory beneath her Avocado Tree. Now she felt a gnawing desire to be busy with work of her own. A transformation seemed to be happening within her, reshaping the roots of her being. For several months, no day had passed without her dedicating a heartfelt dance to her potted vegetation. Yet she longed for a higher purpose for her art.

Somehow, she felt she must have been born for better things than dancing within the four plaster walls of her two-room apartment.

———◆———

She found herself lifted in the freight elevator of an old factory by a large, bullish, long-haired, blue-jeaned woman operator who answered only in "Nods and Becks and wreathed Smiles, such as hang on Hebe's cheek and love to live in dimple sleek." She entered the top-floor loft from the freight elevator and discovered an artist's studio. The studio, littered with clear or green polyester resin sculptures of women's breasts filled with fish and bubbling water, harbored about twelve naked women. They were arranged around the center of the floor in white plastic, simulated leather, beanbag chairs, soft, amorphous furnishings that mold to the languishing body. Each was naked, and each held a pink plastic object in her hand. The object was shaped like an overgrown tube of lipstick, with the lipstick erect.

"Hi! If you've come for the workshop, you've missed the lecture," said a short-haired woman of about forty.

"I have? You mean, I'm late?" gulped Dorissa apprehensively, amid the bubbling breasts of tropical fish tanks and naked women that greeted her eyes. "I thought I was supposed to be here at seven-thirty."

"No, seven. That was a misprint in *Majority Voice*. But come in anyway, sister. Sit down and join us," answered the leader of the group. "We are just about to begin some actual body work. You can put your clothes over there on the coat rack."

"This is sure to be a weird night," thought Dorissa, "but at least I'm not sitting home waiting for Noah." She hesitated a moment, almost deciding to turn and run for the freight elevator, which she heard descending into the floor behind her. "This is the Body-consciousness-expanding Workshop, isn't it?" she asked with even more feigned innocence than she intended.

"Yes, of course. I'm Narcissa Tittel. Please take off your clothes and join us," answered the woman in a tone that showed she was becoming a little impatient to get on with her job. "We don't want to waste any time!"

51

Dorissa didn't really know what to do, but she felt sufficiently intimidated to obey. She removed her pant-suit, pantyhose, and stretch bikini underwear, and told herself that it was really no different from undressing for a sauna at a gym. Then she sat in an empty white beanbag next to a rather pretty brunette whose right arm, thrown over her chest and shoulder, covered what it could of her protruding breasts. The brunette, whose legs were crossed to hide her pubis, seemed less at ease than others in the group, who lay back, with their eyes half closed, and began to run their own hands slowly over their bodies.

"You'll find your vibrator in a sanitary plastic bag beside your chair, dear," said Narcissa to Dorissa.

"Right here," said the ill-at-ease brunette, whispering to Dorissa and pointing to the object referred to as a vibrator by Narcissa. "It's my first time, too," she added, whispering confidentially. "I have to bite my tongue to keep from laughing."

"Now, sisters," said Narcissa, "lie back in your beanbags and close your eyes and think about centuries of sexual repression. . . . Think how men have been 'beating the bishop' together for years . . . jerking off at stag parties together to see who could come first, while we've been chained to the scrub brushes and washboards, and now the vacuum cleaners and washing machines of America, afraid to even look and see what was between our legs! Think how we've been socialized never to touch ourselves or know what pleasure our bodies can give us, and then relax, sisters, and feel your sensual being. Feel it flow over you in sensation . . . let it fill your pores with freedom, and breathe, very deeply . . ." said Narcissa, sinking back in her chair and slowly beginning to run her hands over her breasts and stomach. "Touch yourselves, sisters, and see what nice soft creatures we are. . . . We deserve to enjoy our bodies," she continued, in a trance. Then she began tickling her nipples with her fingers and breathing deeply so that her tanned and slightly rounded belly rose and fell beneath her ministering hands.

"It's too funny! I can't stand it!" whispered the brunette, turning around in her beanbag and burying her face in her hands to smother a giggle.

Dorissa still didn't know what to do, but she was not in the mood to finger her own nipples. She was intimidated enough by the sea of fingering bodies to wonder if she had missed something important in Narcissa's lectures. On the wall behind Narcissa, she noticed a chart of the female genitalia with a large red arrow marking "The Clitoris." To the left of the female anatomy was a chart marked "The Tittel Deluxe Vibrator." The "On" switch was marked with another red arrow.

"I guess the red arrows are where it's at," suggested Dorissa to the brunette, who stopped her silent giggling long enough to nod affirmatively to Dorissa.

"Well," said Dorissa, "I don't know if I can. Can you?"

"Definitely not *here*," whispered the brunette, quite emphatically, between silent giggles, snorts, and guffaws. "Got any ideas?"

Narcissa Tittel panted from her beanbag, "Are you beginning to moisten, sisters? Are your glands beginning to secrete their marvelous juices? Are you beginning to feel a tingle in your groins? If so, wonderful! If not, you can use a little saliva like this to reduce the friction at first, or you may want to insert the smooth fingerlike vibrator into the vagina, gently, like this," she added in a deepening tone as she deftly demonstrated exactly what she meant, first wetting her finger in her mouth and then inserting the jiggling pink plastic device between the lips of her revealed vulva.

"*Madre mia*," thought Dorissa, eyes bulging at the ease with which the women, except for the brunette beside her, followed Narcissa's instructions, writhing a little in their chairs with self-involvement. "Times have really changed since I was a girl fending off Salvatore Carboratore in the back seat of his rebuilt Chevy, wondering whether I had a bone blocking my vagina!"

"What shall I do?" whispered the brunette. "I really want to get out of here, but I *don't* want to let myself in for a lot of rhetoric if I get up to go."

"I want to go, too," whispered Dorissa. "It's too much for me. I've got an idea!" She whipped her battery-driven, transistorized, cassette tape recorder out of her huge bottomless pocketbook and pressed the "On" button. "I could do with turning on a little sensual music, if no one objects, Ms. Tittel," she said.

53

"Whatever turns you on, sister," said Narcissa.

"It puts me into an *absolute trance*," answered Dorissa assuringly. Then she began to move in her chair in the rhythm of the dance music that played from the recorder. "Just dance if you can," whispered Dorissa to the brunette. "We'll dance right out of here."

"Anything to get out of following instructions," answered the brunette. "*Automatic auto*-eroticism is too redundant for my taste!" she added leering at the pink vibrator in her hand.

Dorissa got up from her white beanbag chair and glided into the corner of the room, where she began to belly dance in a feigned trancelike movement, as if totally involved in her senses. The brunette, who stood up to join her, revealed that she was a rather tall and shapely, well-endowed woman who, when not attempting to hold back a guffaw, was quite pretty—even beautiful.

"You belly dance rather well," she whispered to Dorissa beneath the strains of the taped Middle Eastern music emanating from the tiny recorder.

"So do you, come to think of it!" said Dorissa, having opened her half-closed eyes for a better look at the dancing brunette undulating before her.

"Well, I haven't belly danced in years," sighed the woman, leaning closer in a snake-armed pose and looking very Egyptian.

"What do you mean, 'in years'?" asked Dorissa with interest. "Have you belly danced before? You look like a pro at it."

"Yes, I used to dance all the time," answered the gyrating brunette.

"Really? As a hobby?" Dorissa became more interested.

"No, I danced professionally, in the Phoenician Garden on Eighth Avenue, about fifteen years ago, when it first opened. Let's get out of here and I'll tell you all about it!"

"Okay, just keep belly dancing, because it looks like they are really getting into themselves and will hardly notice that we aren't with them!"

Dorissa and the brunette, who offered her name as "Delila Dandi," performed a sexy duet. In fact, the burning Arabic embers in Delila's eyes inspired Dorissa to dance more sensuously.

Many of the lounging, lolling, vibrating women turned to

watch them belly dance. Pink and plump, light-auburn-haired Dorissa did a stomach-fluttering Belly Roll, while tall, tanned, slender, dark-haired Delila leaned toward her doing the Shoulder Shake.

Lift the hands and arms outward at shoulder level. Move one shoulder and then the other forward and back in rapid alternation so that the breasts shimmy from side to side.

Delila's smooth and rounded protuberances shook in front of Dorissa's own jiggling breasts; as Delila danced, turning this way and that, her body almost came bumpity-bump, warm, round, and flat, up against Dorissa's.

"I'm getting so excited by this music!" said Delila. "I haven't danced in years, and it feels good!" Her smile was radiant. "They're all watching us! I think we're turning them on," she whispered. "Let's give them a real show and drive them crazy!"

"Okay," said Dorissa.

"Here goes!" said Delila, shimmying her breasts.

Dorissa and Delila danced like two snakes, and then like two swans courting each other. They would pass this way and that, very close, almost grazing nude body with nude body, but not quite touching. It was a performance Dorissa did well, but without real involvement, though she noticed that Delila was getting into it. Delila hip-bumped to the white beanbags they'd occupied and picked up the two vibrators that had been assigned to them. Turning on the pink plastic devices, she held them high over her head so that her hands fluttered with their vibrations.

"It's The Dance of the Pink Vibrators!" she whispered, handing Dorissa one of them, and showing her how to dance very suggestively with it, first making as if to insert it between her own thighs and then between the thighs of her partner.

"Oh sisters, sisters!" sighed Narcissa Tittel, moving her vibrator against her vulva even more quickly, it seemed, than the vibrator could vibrate. "This is a terrific addition to our workshop! Just go with it, sisters. Get off on it!" Narcissa Tittel continued to titillate herself as she watched Dorissa and Delila belly dance suggestively, moving their breasts and hips in twin rhythms and pressing their vibrators to each other's navels. "What a turn-on! We should have this sort of thing more often in the workshop. This is super!" Narcissa added, tensing wildly and then releasing herself in a groan against her beanbag chair, her pink vibrator falling to the floor with a little thud, where it continued to dance all by itself, around and around on the fuzzy rug.

"Ahhhhh, it was great! Come again, sisters. That will be ten dollars, please!" she told Delila and Dorissa as they excused themselves early from the workshop. Plunking their money down, as the other women began to devour wine and cheese snacks provided by Narcissa, they dressed in a sweated hurry and made their way down the freight elevator and into the street.

"Boy, am I glad to be out of there!" laughed Delila.

"Well, some of what Narcissa Tittel said made sense," mused Dorissa.

"Of course," agreed Delila, "I'm all for lifting the ugly hand of repression off the buttocks of the female, but automatic auto-eroticism is boring as hell! I've tried it long before Narcissa Tittel came along with her workshop, and it just doesn't do a thing for me. I only visited out of intellectual curiosity. I'm a sociologist of sorts, and the phenomenon of battery-driven, transistorized, orgiastic consciousness-raising may very well be unprecedented in the history of human endeavor!" she laughed, this time quite loudly. "Isn't it great not to have to whisper?"

"I hope it is unprecedented and stays that way!" said Dorissa. "It's an ecological disaster."

"A what? I suppose you'd approve if they used organic bananas or cucumbers instead," interjected Delila with a characteristic giggle.

"Well, it would be better than all that plastic pollution," said Dorissa a little too seriously for Delila not to be thoroughly amused by her.

"Are you serious?" asked Delila.

"Let's talk about belly dancing instead," answered Dorissa.

Soon Dorissa found herself seated before the roaring fireplace of Delila Dandi's penthouse on Central Park West. She was whisked there in a cab by Delila, who insisted on having a cozy talk over a warm brandy snifter rather than stand chatting on the cold corner of Mercer Street, in the last frost of winter.

Dorissa discovered that Delila Dandi was actually Delila Dandi's real name. Delila was the name given her by her Greek-Jewish grandmother, and Dandi had been shortened from Dandilininski by her Polish-Romanian grandfather when he immigrated to America two generations earlier. She had been one of the first belly dancers in New York City's famed Phoenician Garden fifteen years before when she'd danced, working her way through graduate school to earn a doctorate in sociology.

"It was a big deal in those days! I got lots of publicity from the newspapers on the angle of being a belly dancing college girl," she laughed, brushing the whole thing aside with a wave of her hand, as if it were the most ordinary thing in the world.

The Veil Dance

The vivacious Delila Dandi was the founder and executive director of a computerized firm called Lovemakers, Inc., a refined and detailed dating service that matched people to the teeth. The couples matched by Lovemakers, Inc., were often so identical they looked and even sounded alike, which usually resulted in "love" at first sight and a union that had great lasting power. Her motto was "You can only see yourself as being as happy as you see yourself as being." It was the kind of non sequitur she always threw out at the rabble and the sort of clever quip that kept her rolling in dough. She was a believer in the power of positive thinking and a member of "the human potential" branch of sociology.

Delila never, of course, used her dating service to find her own mates, because the only thing that turned her on was the process of getting to know someone she might not end up getting along with. She needed the challenge of unchartered territory. She did not want to spend her evenings talking with someone who liked what she liked. She would rather be introduced to something she didn't like and knew nothing about, in hopes of expanding her horizons. That was why she'd had the idea of creating the first computerized dating service in the world. Her firm had grown to be the most venerable institution of its kind. Delila made a great living from it. She arranged dates between jet setters, matching America's social-climbing *nouveau riche* with what was left of the world's shrinking aristocracy. The substantial income she made from the New York and California branches served to decrease her inferiority complex about having been "born in the gutter."

Though Delila was far more worldly and wealthy than Dorissa, the two women soon found they had a lot in common. Delila, like Dorissa, had come from a poor immigrant background, a cultural identity she shared with a sense of transcendent pride. Delila, moreover, had a personality that glittered with a positive, smiling aura. She had such faith in her dreams of romance and pleasure that Dorissa found herself believing in them just by being near her.

Dorissa sat again one evening on Delila's plush lion-skinned sofa and expostulated on her theories of the belly dance, which she now called The Birth Dance of Earth. She spoke with enthusiasm to Delila. "Originally, the primitive dancer probably entered naked beneath her veil. Then, after removing it and dancing up a frenzy, she went into the "birth mime" position, kneeling in a backbend and working her stomach in birth contractions, the magic hocus-pocus that caused birth."

"Oh yes," mused Delila, sipping her glass of Chartreuse liqueur, "what we called the floorwork at the Pheonician Garden is probably the remnant of the ancient birth mime."

Dorissa stood up and leaned back slowly rolling her belly, until she rested the top of her head on the floor behind her.

"Yes, it's a very sexually inviting position," said Delila Dandi, licking the edge of her liqueur glass with the tip of her tongue. "I'm just reminded of a quote I saw reproduced on a statue of Isis when I visited Egypt last year: 'I am that which is, has been, and shall be. My veil no one has lifted. The fruit I bore was the sun. . . .' or something like that."

"Wow! Incredible! Fits with my idea of the veil dance as a sa-

59

cred ritual to the Earth goddess!" Dorissa jumped up and sat again on the sofa.

"Yes, to lift the veil of Isis is to discover the secret of life, the Eleusinian Mysteries!" drawled Delila, slowly lifting her panty-hosed feet from the glass coffee table and tucking them under Dorissa's bottom.

"Dance for me now . . . orgiastic birth mime and all," Delila insisted. "I'd love to see you do your thing! I'll fetch a nice gossamer veil from the back of my closet where it's been for ten years and you can dance, *purely*, ritualistically, here in front of the fireplace—naked as an Egyptian priestess! It will be fun!"

"Oh yes!" agreed Dorissa, all wrapped up in Eleusinian Mysteries.

"You see, dahling, to be a primitive in our civilization, one has to be *awfully sophisticated*. It's a dreadful paradox, isn't it? But never mind, you'll manage," comforted Delila, putting a thoughtful arm around Dorissa's shoulder. "We'll turn out the lights and let the fire glow like the altar of a pagan temple."

Delila lay half sprawled, a sultan, upon the pillows of her sofa watching intently as Dorissa, having undressed, floated into the enormous living room, with Delila's veil caressing her torso and arms. She danced toward Delila, peering over the edge of her veil, the firelight behind her silhouetting her body.

"Marvelous! A true fertility rite," murmured Delila as Dorissa danced toward her, revealing her nakedness.

Hold the veil in back of you so that it closes around you in front, and then swing veil in circles around your head and body by lifting one arm and then the other over your head.

Dorissa danced nimbly, and Delila grew more intent as the orgasmic climax of the dance climbed to a frenzied height.

"A sensual rite!" Delila exclaimed softly from her sultanic position on the sofa. "If I were a man I would surely want to fuck you. *Sublime* eroticism."

"With the female as *active* agent of her *own sexuality*," gasped Dorissa as she glided, dipped, and spun around to a finish, ringing her finger cymbals over her head.

Delila leaped up from the sofa, took Dorissa in her arms, and gave her a giant kiss on the mouth. "That was lovely, dahling. Simply lovely!" she sighed. Then she led Dorissa to the glass doors of the terrace overlooking Central Park. "Look," she whispered into Dorissa's ear, "the moon has the face of a woman in ecstasy."

Dorissa looked up at what, to her, seemed to be the glowing white navel of the sky, set like a jewel in its dark belly. Above the penthouse terrace, planted with trees and shrubbery, the moon was, indeed, full and showing its mysterious features like a Rorschach test. "Delila Dandi is the most romantic person I've ever met!" she thought to herself.

"I haven't listened to my old records in years. I like them better now after watching *you* dance to them. It makes me feel like dancing, too," laughed Delila.

"Why don't you? . . . here in front of the firelight! The moon is full. Time for all pagan witches to perform their sacred rites to the Moon goddess!" said Dorissa, with the enthusiasm of a child creating a world of make-believe.

"You're *right*," smiled Delila, "absolutely right!" She unzipped her black velvet hip-huggers, unbuttoned her red silk blouse, and slipped off her bikini panties. "I have a feeling we once knew each other in the ancient past. We were both dancing priestesses of Diana, gypsy worshipers of the Moon." Delila took up the veil and wrapped it around her body so that her breasts and erected nipples and dark pubic hair showed through the sheerness of the cloth.

Dorissa was inebriated by her own exuberant dancing. Her knees felt weak. She reclined on the sofa and sank down into its cushions, propping her head on one hand so that she could watch Delila. Delila belly danced in front of Dorissa, leaning her sheerly covered breasts over Dorissa's face as seductively as a Salome. She slowly opened and closed her veil so that her naked body was shown in a shimmer of firelight. She shook her breasts, rolled her belly, and swayed her hips.

Dorissa had a vision of leaping up in pursuit of her. It was a sort of animal, aggressive urge that she'd never felt before. It surfaced from her buried longings. Now she comprehended, all at once, as if she were for a moment male, the soft temptation of a woman's body, the inviting delight of a woman's belly. She

61

thought how the hunger for satisfaction in the male must be direct and unbearable, a thrust for power, and an immediate desire for gratification.

Suddenly she pitied men, understood their wars. All at once she knew how unbearable it must be to be a man, dependent on the whims of the female, teased by the delicate beauty of a creature whose rounded, smooth, and inviting body was a mystery like the Moon's—satiny, peachlike, pearlike, and sweetly acid, like a tempting orange hidden within its attractive skin.

"No wonder John the Baptist lost his head to Salome," she thought. "No wonder men felt the need to enslave women in harems at the fall of the matriarchate." Dorissa lay like a sultan, hypnotized by a dancing woman. Then, breaking out of her mesmerization, she began dancing also. She moved like Delila in a frenzy.

"You don't like being teased, do you, Little Isis?" said Delila, taking Dorissa by the arms and kissing her on the mouth. She pulled Dorissa down on the couch. Both women were sweating from the exertion of dancing. Their hair was damp and smelled of delicate feminine perfumes.

When Delila began caressing her nipples, Dorissa could not resist her. They were her Achilles heel, and she responded immediately to the delicate gestures of Delila's lips. There seemed to be an electrical current running from her nipples to her groin, which began aching as her vagina began to water like a mouth awaiting a sumptuous feast.

"Don't you want to feel my tongue on you like this, Little Isis?" whispered Delila, wiggling the wet tip of it on Dorissa's open palm.

When Delila's finger gently found its way inside of her, causing her to sigh deeply, Dorissa felt no reason to resist the soft pleasure. There was nothing harsh or heavy about the way Delila handled her body.

"Oh honey, you're so wet and ready. No woman has ever excited me so much. You're all juicy and you smell delicious." Delila continued to murmur, sniffing the finger she had inserted between Dorissa's vulva. She ran her smooth, soft palm over

Dorissa's belly. "You feel exactly like warm satin," she told Dorissa. "Let me lick you. I want to make you feel so good."

Dorissa had never before had a lover as verbal as Delila. She admired Delila's abandon. Suddenly, Dorissa was annoyed with her own sociological inhibitions. She wanted to be free of the psychological yoke that bound her.

Delila silently slid down and placed her tongue on Dorissa's clitoris. Dorissa's anxiety crept back again. "I can't," she whispered.

"Of course you can. I'll teach you. You'll see," insisted Delila. "Just relax and feel my tongue on you, like this." She licked Dorissa again. "I'm not going to stop, darling, no matter what. Take as long as you need to. I'm just going to keep on, gently, *steadily*, until you feel so good."

Dorissa felt electricity begin to quiver within her and after several minutes of supreme sensation, she felt an unbearable surge of pleasure washing through her thighs and belly. Perhaps it was Delila's insistent determination, or perhaps it was her gentle touch. Whatever the reason, Dorissa experienced a longer and more powerful orgasm than she had ever known. Dorissa let out an animal groan that seemed to release demons from her.

"Don't be afraid. I've got you," said Delila, hugging Dorissa firmly.

Then a flood of uncontrollable tears was released from Dorissa's eyes, and she wept quietly in Delila's arms.

"So, Little Isis," said Delila softly, "we meet again, thousands of years later, and rediscover our Eleusinian Mysteries."

"What a tremendous power, this wonderful power of being woman," thought Dorissa. Before she left she had learned to reciprocate the pleasure Delila had given her. She'd experienced Delila's *enormous* capacity for multiple orgasmic release and sheer sensual pleasure. For such feminine love-making, Morman Failer, the famous, *machismo* American novelist, might wish he were a woman. Such heavenly tenderness! Delila was an expert muff-diver, an artist of cunnilingus, a master of nipples, a princess of the pubes, a Venus of the mound, a Penelope of endurance, a gratified gratifier. She was as soft as a mothering bosom and as comforting. Delila had made Dorissa more satisfied to be a woman than ever before.

She also convinced Dorissa that Pat Campley was right. *The medium was, indeed, the message—even in sexuality!* Making love with a feminine woman was a masculine experience. Making love with a masculine man was a feminine experience. With a woman one could be gentle, controlled, and aggressive, all at once. With a man, one needed to resist just a little, be less aggressive, be soft and receptive and not mind being manhandled. There was a small degree of sadism and masochism within the norm of heterosexuality. As a woman, she'd allowed her aggressive feelings to be squelched. Remaining healthy would require keeping a delicate balance of aggression and passivity in her nature. Breaking her douche bag in Oliver's face had been the first glimmer of health she'd experienced.

Delila convinced Dorissa that she should risk getting some notoriety by staging her own dance demonstration near the heart of the capitalist exchange, Wall Street.

"What do you mean?" Dorissa asked innocently.

"Well, darling, you just put on your dancing costume and bring your cassette recorder and start dancing in Battery Park, every afternoon at lunchtime, until Wall Street gathers to watch. Close behind the crowd the newsmen will follow, and you'll be made, American media style!"

Dorissa thought of Battery Park, the little park adjacent to Wall Street, where ferry boats docked and sailed off to take their sight-seeing cruise of the harbor's Statue of Liberty. All she needed was to think of that Great Mother symbol of freedom to convince her that Delila was right. She would do it.

When Dorissa arrived at her apartment she found Noah waiting, angry with worry.

"Where on Earth have you been? I'm beside myself. You said to meet you here hours ago." He paced the floor as she calmly removed her coat and hung it in the closet.

"Oh Noah," she sighed, about to fabricate an excuse. Then taking him by the hand, she confessed her meeting and rendezvous with Delila Dandi.

Noah was at first shocked, then hurt by her confession, but older and wiser than she, he was tolerant. He suppressed his jealousy in hopes that her infatuation with the glamorous jet-set woman would pass. His experience with Dorissa and his knowledge of her background made him quite sure that she was heterosexual, and he knew that many women, as a result of sexual liberation and changing morality, were exploring love with each other in hopes of accepting themselves. "Well, my dear, I believe you really need a man to make you feel complete as a woman. I don't condone what you are doing, but please spare me the details of this little affair you've experienced and I'm sure it will all pass." He loved Dorissa like a daughter despite his sexual feelings for her. He did not want to lose her to anyone else, but didn't feel really threatened by a woman as he would have by a man.

His kind understanding endeared him all the more to her and she resolved not to give him up for Delila, but to play out the drama to see where it would lead. "Oh Noah, you are so wise and good. Forgive me if I've hurt you. I don't want to hurt you, but Delila makes me feel the balance of my own power. She's a woman like me, but so much more self-assertive and in control of her own life. I've been so emotionally dependent on Oliver for so many years, so in need of his approval, and then he pulled the rug out from under me with his philandering. He made me feel inferior, powerless, rejected. Now I feel sorry for him. He's just a man, like most men, robbed of his emotional expressiveness by a need to be tough, firing the stray bullets of his sperm, thoughtlessly exploding seed pods by the force of Mother Nature, a slave to his organ! You are different, of course, so much more sensitive and understanding than most men, but I realize that I've felt inferior to you, too. I've envied you your social power as much as I've envied Oliver's. Now I wouldn't give up my magical clitoris for anything! Not even a glorious penis!" She sighed in exaltation.

"I understand, my dear, but I'm a little worried about your emotional state. This relationship you have begun with this creature could prove to be a distraction that will completely set you off balance. Lesbianism is not so easily condoned by society. It is a risk and can be very painful!" He put on his coat to go home. He was exhausted by the night of worry and the emotional shock. He wanted to be at home, secure amid his own books and memorabilia, where he could think.

"Noah, please don't worry about me. I'm a big girl. I mean, I'm a woman. I know I prefer making love with a man, but Delila makes me feel like taking risks. She makes me feel free to dance and take myself seriously. No wonder most of the world's great adventurers have been men. Women have been conditioned to avoid risk. Besides, the more emotionally secure I feel on the inside, the crazier I seem on the outside." She kissed him good night. "I still love you, Noah, but I don't want to give a damn what anyone else thinks of me, so long as I feel I'm doing what is right!"

She was learning to think like a politician. Meeting a sharp, clever, and successful woman, in the person of Delila Dandi, helped her to realize that she need not greet the world with her weeping woman's heart prominently on her sleeve. She could shimmy her brain as well as she had learned to shimmy her hips. What her father had taught her from the depths of his tenacious immigrant soul emerged in her character.

"If you really want something, you put everything aside, even a cool ice on a hot day, to get it!" If he had given her an inferiority complex about being female, he'd managed to stir enough European immigrant tenacity into her personality to salvage her potential.

Her Avocado Tree, moreover, was giving her a new kind of vegetable sense. She realized that her belief in the robust, life-giving Earth Mother was perhaps more rational than believing in a God crucified by the inhuman greed of men, a God who had to rise above Earth to be divine.

She felt all these thoughts not in words, but in the exhausted muscles and post-orgasmic relaxation of her body as she fell asleep under the watchful gaze of her thoughtful Avocado Tree. She knew now her mission was to help the women of America see that the Earth, herself, was the source of all life, and life its own reason for being. She'd have to risk everything to accomplish her mission. If she wasn't willing to risk all, she might just as well have let the Mack truck do her in.

STEP 8:

The Earth Roll

The noontime sun blazed down over New York Harbor. Cumulus clouds floated through an unusually blue sky. The Statue of Liberty, against a yellowish horizon of pollution, stood coppery green in the sunlight. She raised her torch of freedom over the murky waters off the banks of Battery Park. People on their lunchtime breaks from the offices of Wall Street strolled with senior citizens, mothers with baby carriages, derelicts, junkies, and drug addicts, along the park's asphalt pathways. At the edge of the park overlooking the water was Castle Clinton, a National Monument from the War of 1812, a fortress turned theater where singer Jenny Lyn, the century before, had charmed her New York audience, including Walt Whitman.

In front of the rotund stone structure with its wrought-iron battlements stood Dorissa Femfunelli, daughter of Italian immigrants, her tape recorder in one hand and canvas bag with finger cymbals in the other. Beside her stood the vivacious Delila Dandi, smiling broadly.

"Perfect weather for an Earth ritual, dahling!"

Dorissa was worried. "Are you sure this is a good idea, Delila? I may get arrested for indecent exposure or something!"

"Oh baby doll! Look at that teeny bopper with her cheeks hanging out of her denim shorts! This is the twentieth century, starring *Tits 'n' Ass* on Broadway! Hardly anyone is going to have as many clothes on as you do this hot day of spring. The only thing you expose, sweetie, is your adorable belly, and you're only going to do that for a second, at the end of your dance. All we want to do is tease up a crowd this first day. Now give me your robe and I'll go stand over behind that tree. You just go to it and I'll hold back any disturbing weirdos!"

Dorissa flicked her switch and began to dance. It wasn't long before a few Wall Street brokers, with their secretaries, out for lunch; two derelicts; three mothers with plastic and aluminum strollers full of babies munching pizza; and a junkie or two stopped to gather in front of her. Delila winked and gave her the okay sign from her post by the tree, but Dorissa's knees kept wobbling under her chiffon skirts.

"What ya' doin', honey?" chortled one derelict as he stuffed a bottle of wine into the saggy back pocket of his tattered trousers.

Dorissa didn't answer, as Delila had suggested. She just continued slowly feigning estatic involvement. In order to create a sense of mystery, she had taped a long veil dance of eerie music.

"Wait until a big crowd gathers before you flash your tummy!" Delila had commanded earlier as they drove downtown in her convertible.

According to one of the laws of social physics, a small crowd attracts a larger crowd. Soon Dorissa was surrounded by seventy or eighty people, who in turn attracted seventy or eighty more. Twenty minutes later, two hundred or more people—mostly Wall Street executives—crowded to get a view of the oddly ecstatic, sweating, but voluptuous woman who "danced her guts out," swirling her veils, clinking her cymbals, and rolling her gossamer-veiled belly for the benefit of whoever happened along.

Delila watched intently, scheming all the while. As soon as Dorissa's routine came to a final and climactic end, and the wild cheers of the crowd subsided, Delila leaped up on a bench and shouted: "Will you be back again tomorrow at noon, same time, same place?"

Dorissa, as instructed, shouted back in the loudest voice she could manage: "Tomorrow. Same time! Same place!"

Except for a few catcalls from derelicts or a few mouthy invitations from brokers, the crowd had been generally peaceful. There had been a little shoving to get a clearer view of the strange dancer, but otherwise all had gone smoothly.

Delila ran quickly to Dorissa's side. She threw her robe over her, grabbed up the tape player, and ushered the exhausted dancer through the crowd to the ladies' rest room of Castle Clinton. "You were terrific! We'll hide in here until the crowd disperses," she said, dragging Dorissa into one of the pay toilet stalls and locking the door behind them. "We'll come back again tomorrow and give them the same show!" Her hand went up Dorissa's skirt. "Oh, baby, your dancing turns me on," she whispered.

"Delila, please don't call me 'baby.' You sound like a male *chauvinist!* I'm a grown woman, not a baby!"

"I know you are, sweetie. That's why you smell so delicious," said Delila, sniffing her fingers. "Tomorrow I'll do that first so I can smell you on my hand while I watch you dance."

"You're incredible!"

Delila was a new experience. Dorissa hadn't been made love to by a female since her junior high-school days when she and her girlhood friend, Constance Germano, had played boyfriend and girlfriend in the attic. They would hide in the attic corner and pretend to be lovers out on a date, giggling and thrilling over the things they said to each other.

Earlier, in Dorissa's childhood, there had been a girl named Arla Rivers, who lived upstairs. Little seven-year-old Arla liked to play a special game with Dorissa. They'd go down to the cellar, behind the coal bin, tickle each other, and make believe they were Cinderella and the prince *after* the wedding. Dorissa did not know exactly what the game was all about, but it felt good to

have Arla rub her "little red button." Dorissa had not redis-
covered her clitoris until many years later, when she learned its
Latin name and decided to encourage Oliver to play with it.

With Delila's assistance, Dorissa danced for six days at noontime in Battery Park. Delila was expert at fending off undesirables
and fast-talking the policeman who wandered by to check out the
proceedings. She showed them the Parks Department permit she
had managed to acquire by pulling a few strings in the city government. The permit allowed Dorissa to give a free public dance
performance in the park. There was nothing the police could do
to stop her from filling the public place with a crowd for her
noontime performance. Each day Dorissa acquired a larger group
of regular admirers from the offices of Wall Street.

Dorissa became the topic of discussion of coffee breaks and
lunch hours. All the men of Wall Street were speculating as to
whether she would ever remove her veil altogether for more than
a brief flash of her belly. Delila always dragged Dorissa off immediately after her performance and hid her to keep her from
answering questions. She wanted to build a myth around the
mysterious dancer of Battery Park so that Wall Street would become curiouser and curiouser. Only *after* the crowd dissipated and
Dorissa changed into street clothes and dark glasses did they leave
the ladies' rest room.

As the seventh lunchtime arrived, a giant crowd gathered. The
day had been carefully planned to fall on "blue Monday," when
office workers, after the demise of their barbecued, suburban free-
doms, face their forty-hour weeks with weekend hangovers. The
crowd today was different from the crowds before. Today it was
peppered throughout with people carrying cameras and portable
video equipment—reporters, photographers, newsmen, and gossip
columnists. Talk of Dorissa had been spreading throughout the
media during the week. A morning edition of the *Daily News* had
carried a second-page spread about the mysterious belly dancer of
Battery Park who flashed her notorious navel every noontime.
Even though most of the strollers surrounding her in the pictures
wore less clothes than she, her magic navel seemed to be a center of attraction.

Dorissa stood, just as she had for six days, in front of the battlements of Castle Clinton at noon sharp. But instead of flipping her usual switch and starting her dance, she pulled a transistorized megaphone, supplied by Delila, from out of her large canvas bag and began talking instead:

"Today, right here on the grass of Battery Park, we are going to celebrate the Earth Mother with her own sacred ritual dance. We're going to pay tribute to woman as the first human link in the food chain of life, woman as ruler of the vaginal vegetal world!" she declared. She gave a brief history of the degradation of the sacred birth dance, paralleling it with a history of the devolution of the female. She delivered a diatribe against everything from litter to pop-top cans, dogshit to dying whales, dirty politics to plutonium waste, napalm, and air pollution. She declared her New Dance of Liberation as the quintessential feminine celebration of birth and earth and the living counterpart of the male war dance. Noah, much against his will and judgment, had helped her compose her speech the evening before. It was a combination of his intellect and her ardent feeling. She topped it off with her favorite quote from Isadora Duncan: "The dancer of the future will dance the freedom of woman . . . the highest intelligence in the freest body!" She shouted with infectious enthusiasm, and the crowd responded with a burst of applause.

Then flipping her switch, she began to dance more seductively than ever before. Several policemen had not been long in arriving on the scene. They made up the rear of the biggest crowd she had yet assembled. The police stood, arms folded behind their backs, eyes fixed on what they could see of Dorissa as she waved her green veils on the green in front of the antique stone battlements of Castle Clinton.

Dorissa's week of practice had given her the nerve to dance in complete trance with the music. The crowd, which now occupied too large a portion of the small park, pushed and shoved, as parade watchers do, to get a peek at the phenomenon that attracted the heads in front of them. Mothers held babies on their shoulders, and brokers stood on tiptoes in their polished leather shoes to have a better view. A few derelicts lay on the ground and peeked through the legs of the crowd in order to watch the unleashed energy of Dorissa's dance.

This time, instead of just flashing her belly when she ended the veil dance, she flung her veil aside and began to undulate her torso in the agony of a birth mime. Those who didn't understand what she was doing thought she looked rather "sexy" as she descended bare-midriffed to the grassy earth and began to roll around on it, like some peach just lost to a mound of earth from its bobbing branch.

Her body felt ecstasy, naked movement, rhythm, what the sea is about, what trees in the wind are about, what hands of leaves applaud as they clap together or nestle in each other, rustling vein to vein. She felt alive, physical, and real, body *and* visceral soul, dancing barefoot upon the grassy turf, beneath sky and sunlit clouds, like a primitive priestess. A tongue-tied girl from George Washington High School's twirling squad was at last set free from the stiff gait of her marching boots and the breast buckles of her uniform, free from egging the football team on to glory. Her urge for life communicated itself to the crowd, filling the park with human electricity. But just as she rose up from the earth, totally involved in her climactic and orgiastic moment, the hook on her beaded bra broke, and the costume fell to the ground, exposing her breasts to the many eyes of the crowd, including its policemen.

Be free, high priestess! Dance as you did long ago in Eleusis, said the trees of Battery Park to Dorissa's body as she danced on, never noticing that her breasts bobbed naked or that the police were making their way toward her through the hips and elbows of the cheering crowd. As she spun around, one of her weighty Turkish finger cymbals slipped from her finger. In the full velocity of her sweeping turn it sailed like a metal boomerang through the air, beaning a large policeman exactly in the temple and felling him like Goliath. Seeing their comrade wounded, the blue-uniformed soldiers of the city were even more determined in their arrest of the brazen dancer. As she whirled in the final triumphant moment of her bare-breasted Bacchanalian ritual, they descended upon her, grabbing what they could. The many-headed monster of the crowd went wild working its elbows overtime, heaving its amorphous mass this way and that and spitting fire to get a better view. Dorissa, rudely awakened from her trance, had no idea why the police were grabbing her, until she felt a rough hand graze her unadulterated nipple.

STEP 9:

The Toss and Turn

Delila elbowed her way through the crowd to get close to Dorissa. "This girl might even end up replacing the Stars and Stripes with belly buttons and nipples!" she exclaimed with great expectations as the police dragged the proselytizing priestess to their patrol car. Delila noticed two ladybugs sitting in Dorissa's long, tousled hair. Reaching for them, she shouted, "Look, dahling, two ladybugs. It's a sign of good luck from Ceres, the goddess of gardens!" She knew that mentioning some aspect of the great goddess was the best way to comfort her ardent ritualist. "Don't worry! I'll be along with my lawyers as soon as I can!"

"*Mamma mia!*" gasped Dorissa as she took one of the harvest-saving bugs from her hair. "It is a signal that I'm on the right path! You just don't understand!" she argued breathlessly with the police. "I was performing a sacred ritual dance for Mother Nature. After all, breasts are the first human link in the food chain."

"Tell it to the judge, sweetheart!" one responded as they

74

handcuffed her to an officer in the back seat of the patrol car. "That was my buddy, Mike, you knocked out cold."

"Sorry," she answered, "but I didn't knock him out, my finger cymbal did." She wondered why she felt so cheerful, on her way to jail for three misdemeanors and a felony: inciting a riot; indecent exposure; resisting arrest; and assaulting an officer of the law. She imagined the spectacle in all the papers, and on television, too, for news cameras had blinked their shutters and videotapes had wound it all up for posterity. But while American families sat glued to the waves of shining screens munching chips and doodles (BHA added), to the ancient rhythms of the pagan Earth ritual, Dorissa herself stood in a precinct line-up amid prostitutes and pimps in the booking room of a Lower East Side police station. She worried about what Oliver, Noah, Chrysta's teacher, her father, and the principal at St. Aloysius would think of her.

She had come to rely, too much, on Noah for emotional support. His sense of propriety about her behavior perturbed her. He didn't respond empathetically when she'd explained that the medium is the message. He did not approve when she claimed that she would be born overnight by Delila's scheme.

"As a nut, maybe, but as an artist of the dance, never!" he'd quipped, cruelly.

"Sometimes an artist who wants to reach many people has to take a big risk to do it!" She tried to gain his empathy. She couldn't tell for sure whether he was jealous of her kinship with Delila, or truly appalled by her park scheme, but he'd stomped out of her apartment the night before, leaving her to finish writing her spiritual speech alone. She had felt as hurt by his disapproval as she had by Oliver's.

But now, somehow, she didn't feel as upset as she might. She felt exhilarated. She'd dared to have public communion with Earth, Herself. She'd released the bird of freedom from her own breast and let it fly beyond the branches of Battery Park. Nothing would stop her now! She'd once again defied the man in her life, Noah, her security blanket, and she felt reborn, a woman, earthy and unafraid.

"The place is too crowded here, and the judge can't set bail for you women until tomorrow," said the officer at the desk. "We're going to have to paddy-wagon you all to Rikers Island for the night."

Dorissa paused in her reveries and noticed that she was being addressed right along with the group of prostitutes crowding the room. Some of them, like herself, had police jackets thrown over their scantily clad bodies. She realized that they must have been caught in a raid of some massage parlor. She looked to her right and caught the eye of a brown-skinned woman who sat beside her on a bench.

"Were you workin' at our place, honey? I don't remember ever seein' you!"

"No, I was arrested in Battery Park!" answered Dorissa, not knowing what else to say to the highly painted, sheerly clad woman.

The woman, in a New York, black Puerto Rican accent, continued the conversation: "Oh that's a bad beat, honey. The cops is tough on girls around there. A lot of secretaries and wives like to keep that Wall Street area clean! Well, looks like we all headed to Rikers for the night! That goddamn hellhole!"

Dorissa began to feel a little worried that Delila had not shown up at the precinct. Dorissa felt quite totally dependent on her new lover to set things right, as promised. Realizing that the officer at the desk took her for one of the ring of prostitutes, she walked over and addressed him in a whisper:

"Officer, excuse me, but I'm not with *them!*"

"I don't care who you're with, sweetheart," he barked, "just keep your behind on the bench until we're ready to move you along!"

Dorissa returned to her seat. Her hands were shaking with frustration.

"What's Rikers Island like?" she asked the brown-skinned, pink-clad woman.

"Oh honey, I can see you is a beginner at this!" laughed the woman. "You got a real treat comin'!"

Delila was feeling a little guilty because she had deliberately pulled some of the threads out of the hooks and eyes on Dorissa's beaded bra just before the performance. "The bigger the ruckus, the better the coverage," she had reasoned. Now she was having trouble contacting her lawyers. She reached the precinct only moments after Dorissa had been paddy-wagoned to Rikers Island.

"Look, lady, we'll take a message for your friend, but we can't guarantee she'll receive it before morning," replied the officer at the desk when she begged him to contact Dorissa and reassure her that help was on the way.

"Tell her I'll be there with my lawyers tomorrow as soon as bail is set," she insisted. Then she indignantly reprimanded the officer for mixing "the high priestess of feminism" with a band of prostitutes. "Someone will pay for this awful error when the mayor's office hears about it!" she threatened.

"Take it easy, lady. Your friend has four counts against her. She ain't exactly the most law-abiding citizen on my books!" he answered wryly.

Noah happened to see the seven o'clock news and was totally dismayed at her bare-breasted arrest. He had deliberately flown to Washington, D.C., under the pretense of working on publicity for the opera's visit to Kennedy Center. He was angry with Dorissa and wanted to be out of town during her wild fiasco. It reminded him of the time his disturbed wife took off her clothes to recite erotic poetry on the Staten Island ferry, and he wasn't sure he was at all ready to stick by Dorissa as he had his insane wife.

Oliver arrived to visit Chrysta at his mother's apartment, to witness Dorissa's bare-breasted performance on his mother's TV screen. He was aghast when Chrysta shouted with glee:

"Look, Daddy, it's Mommy! She's belly dancing on television, but she doesn't have her costume on!"

"She's flipped her lid completely!" Oliver groaned to his mother. He was thinking about what his colleagues at the university would say in the morning. His mother, to no avail, pointed out how well Dorissa handled the reporters who thrust microphones in her face:

"I'm dancing to free women, and you are arresting me for being one!" Dorissa proclaimed on Walter Cronkite's broadcast of the news. "If your shirt fell off in the park, no one would arrest you!" she told one male reporter who questioned her.

77

Delila, at home in front of three portable TVs, sipped Chartreuse liqueur and beamed. She was thrilled at the coverage Dorissa was receiving on all three major networks. Dorissa's proclamation of her belly dance as a ritual celebration of women and the Earth came loud and clear over the din of the crowded park. Delila toasted herself as a veritable genius of a Svengali. As far as she was concerned her superstar was being created before her eyes. She planned to make her Trilby the greatest star of the twentieth century.

At Rikers Island, Dorissa found herself sitting on a prison cot surveying her surroundings: a six-by-four-foot cell with a smooth, concrete floor. Beside the cot was a toilet without a lid or a seat, and a small sink. Through bars, she could see a tiny glimpse of evening sky through a steel-grated window across the corridor from her cell. Her costume had been taken from her. She wore a light green cotton dress that came to a respectable length beneath her knees. She had expected Delila to appear, like her fairy godmother, and set her free. The injured policeman, though recuperated, was definitely pressing charges. When no one had appeared to bail her out, she had been sent with others to the cellblock. The brown-skinned pink-clad woman who shared her cell introduced herself to Dorissa as Juanita Pietri.

"Ain't you got nobody to bail you outa here, honey? Who's your pimp? Or did you get caught turnin' tricks all by your lonesome?" she asked.

"I didn't get arrested for tricks," answered Dorissa, feeling truly anxious as the bleak fact of the jail cell permeated her mood. She tried to act self-assured before the stranger: "I got arrested on five counts; I think they said: disturbing the peace, inciting riot, indecent exposure, and, oh yeah, resisting arrest, and assaulting an officer in the line of duty. The last is a *felony!* Do you happen to know what that means?"

Juanita began to laugh. "You real funny, baby! And you is in big trouble. A *misdemeanor* is *little* shit, but a *felony* is *big* shit; that's all I know! You don't look like no hippy peace nut. You ain't no Cuban nationalist, is you? What kind of honky politics is you into?"

"I'm not in politics at all," answered Dorissa, fighting back the tears that were forming in the corners of her eyes. "I'm just a belly dancer for the Earth Mother."

Juanita laughed again. Dorissa noticed that she had a gold bicuspid. "You really funny, baby! What kind of pitch is that?"

"Well, I guess you could say it's a *feminine* brand of feminism," answered Dorissa, seriously trying to explain herself.

"You mean *women's lib?*" asked Juanita. "Is you one o' them purple-stockin' witches or somethin'? I heard about them."

"No, I'm just a belly dancer, really a birth dancer, for women!"

"Hmmmm, I gonna have to get you to show me some of that!" laughed Juanita. "Where did you take it off, honey?"

Dorissa, feeling very uneasy, simply decided to answer all questions with simple directness. "I took my veil off in Battery Park, at noontime, near Wall Street."

Juanita looked at her for a moment, then became helpless with laughter loud enough to bring the guard from her station at the end of the long cellblock.

"You girls quiet down in there. It's almost lights out. Some people are trying to sleep!" The guard spoke sternly, causing Dorissa's nerves to tingle.

"Oh man, I don't believe you!" Juanita whispered, controlling her laughter. "Takin' your clothes off on Wall Street. That's too much! You must have a few screws missin' topside the head!" She slapped Dorissa on the knee.

Dorissa began to tremble, not sure now that Juanita wasn't right. Sitting in her dark prison cell, just after lights out, Dorissa began to imagine the ramifications of what she'd done: She could see Oliver's disapproving face as it faded into Noah's. She thought of her family. She pictured Uncle Giuseppi shaking his fist at the television screen in fierce, passionate disgust for her lewd behavior. She saw Aunt Raphaela going to church to say novenas for her soul. She saw her mother, Sophia, not sure whether to cry over her daughter's exposure or be thrilled that she was on television. She imagined Chrysta's teacher feeling sorry for Chrysta as she faced the other children in school. She was petrified at what Oliver might do in retaliation. She wondered if Delila had deserted her, and she felt disgusted with herself for having gone along with the wild scheme to media stardom. She'd thought to carry her message of the ancient belly dance and its wholesome benefits to great masses of women. Instead, she found herself lying on a cot in a dark jail. She couldn't help emitting a few stifled sobs into the darkness. Her jailmate, Juanita, could not help feeling sorry for her.

"Now, don't you worry, baby!" she whispered, consoling Dorissa from her own cot across the tiny cell. "I got somethin' here that will fix you right up. I can see you is brand new at doin' time!" In the darkness, Juanita found her shoe beneath the cot, and loosening the inner arch, she extracted two cigarettes from under it. "This is good strong weed, and it will relax you good so you can get some sleep." She lit the cigarette and passed it to Dorissa.

"Thanks, but I don't smoke very much!" said Dorissa, beginning to feel panicky about her lack of contact with the outside world.

"This ain't no ordinary cigarette, honey. Don't tell me you never done grass befo'. Come on now, don't be bashful! It's the best stuff you can get in *this* city. Real strong! You ain't goin' to tell me you don't want my laughin' grass, I hope, 'cause it make you feel good enough to sleep. If the guard smells somethin', I'll take the rap. Come on, now. Take some drags!"

Dorissa felt intimidated by the marijuana Juanita offered. She didn't want to admit to more inexperience than she had already, not if she was going to have to share the cell with her all night. Logic made her a little fearful of the stranger, but psychically she knew Juanita was harmless and meant well.

Juanita proceeded to give her a little advice as to how to get along on "the inside." If Dorissa wanted to stay out of trouble, she was neither to smile nor frown at the guards or inmates. "When they can't read you, they leave you alone!" she explained. "Don't a pretty little thing like you got some friends to bail you out?" she asked, passing the joint to Dorissa in the darkness.

"I don't know what happened to them. They didn't show up! They'll probably be here in the morning, I hope," wept Dorissa, her tears evoked by Juanita's question.

"I served six years already, sweetie, and I survived it." Juanita patted her arm reassuringly and handed her the marijuana again.

Dorissa took a deep drag, forgetting herself for a moment to wonder about Juanita. She had noticed two small scars on her left cheek, but aside from that the woman was handsome. She guessed she was about thirty. She was taller than average and roundly built. She wore her shiny black hair in a very short Afro that surrounded her smooth brown face with tiny ringlets.

When the joint was finished between them, Juanita stretched out on her own cot and began to whisper across the dark cell. The monologue that issued from her as she attempted to distract Dorissa from her trouble, was a mixture of Puerto Rican passion and black humor. She may not have made it farther than Rikers Island, but she had a sharp mind and a full heart.

"Honey, my family's been on welfare fo' three generations. I've been hustlin' the streets fo' bread and love since I was ten, but I ain't lost my soul to no man! They gonna have to cut my heart out befo' I'll ever lose it down the goddamn white toilets of this black hell. Long as I can cry, they ain't got my soul, baby. I seen a hooker after she can't cry no mo'. That's when she's a zombie—one of the livin' dead. But I got lots o' tears in me, which means I can still laugh, too. That is the *holy truth!* My soul, still mine!" she whispered huskily. "You can still cry, too!"

"Too damn easily!" Dorissa replied, falling in with Juanita's mood. She began to feel warmly toward Juanita's disembodied voice in the dark cell.

"You'll learn how to keep yo' soul for yo' own private bank and never cash it in fo' no man. I still got mine, right between my legs, and ain't no man gonna trade me for a *mean* prick! No how."

Dorissa learned that Juanita had run away from her Spanish Harlem home at the age of thirteen after her father had forced her to marry the owner of the local liquor store. The owner was the richest man on the block, and, as it turned out, the most sadistic. He tied her to the bed on their wedding night and virtually raped her. Traumatized, she locked herself in the bathroom. The next morning, when her husband left for work, Juanita fled to Forty-second Street. There she lived in a house with several runaway girls who'd been taken in by a tough pimp called "Loose

Larry." She suffered an illegal abortion at the age of fourteen, only to be arrested a few months later on drug charges.

"I never touch the stuff myself, honey. Never sold it neither. I was just livin' there when they come and raid the place and find three kilos o' snow stashed in my bureau drawer, where Larry kept it. Once he shot me up with junk, and I almost died from it. But I ain't never shot myself up, and I don't want to. A little weed is all I need to get me through my days. I don't even drink rum; no heavy stuff o' no kind! I seen too many women all messed up on junk. That prick, Larry, he dumped the whole mess on me, and I end up servin' time fo' him." Juanita laughed with ironic remorse.

Soon Dorissa was telling her the spiritual saga of her own life and the reasons behind her arrest in Battery Park. She was amazed that Juanita understood better than Noah, Delila, or anyone she'd confided in. Juanita knew exactly why Dorissa wanted to belly dance for the Earth Mother:

"You see, baby," Juanita empathized, "men were created to do the work of the world with their heads, but when God saw he had forgotten somethin', he made women to put some feelin' heart and soul into his work. And his hard mind and her soft heart have got to balance out to keep it all together. Otherwise we all gonna end up in hell. So, it's a good thing you dance for big ole Mama, 'cause she the one who feed the babies and she the one who cook up some rice and beans fo' everybody to eat and somethin' for everybody to dream about. Men just keep wantin' to fly the coup and leave you stuck home with the kids. You know what Bessie Smith say when she sing the blues?" Juanita began to sing very softly and with much soul:

> . . . Lawd I really don't think no man love can last.
> Lawd I don't think no man love can last.
> They'll love you to death then treat you like a thing of the past.
> There's nineteen men livin' in my neighborhood.
> There's nineteen men livin' in my neighborhood.
> Eighteen of them are fools and the one ain't no doggone good.
>
> Lawd, Lawd, Lawd, Lawd, Lawd, O Lawd, Lawd, Lawd,
> That dirty no-good man treats me just like I'm a dog.*

* "Dirty No-Gooder's Blues" by Bessie Smith.

82

"You the bottom of the bottom when you a black Puerto Rican woman. You way, way, way down there, honey, in the basement, with the old newspapers and broken rum bottles. It ain't no comfortable bed. Still, you be lyin' down there on the broken bottles and dirty newspapers, and some guy gonna come along and want to screw you right out of your uncomfortable basement sack, or keep you waitin' there for him to come home nights. So you end up washin' dishes in hell and gettin' screwed fo' the rest o' yo' life."

Juanita sighed deeply, and Dorissa returned her sigh. "Everybody's greedy to get his rocks off, because the government and factory bosses got 'em by the balls, those guys out there, and they gotta take it out on us mamas 'cause we underneath. They hate us for spankin' their asses when they was little boys and we was bigger than them, teachin' them not to mess in their pants. So naturally, now that they is bigger, they gonna give the business to women 'cause they can't give it to each other." Juanita sighed deeply to punctuate her point.

"But lemme tell you, this place wouldn't be so bad, rotten as it is. I mean, ain't no men in here; the ceilin's dry, the toilets flush, they even got hot water, sometime, and three meals a day, bad as they are. You get to read a book or watch an old movie now and then. It would be like a hotel without having to fuck to pay the bill, but they try to get ahold of yo' soul, too. You touch some other woman to make her feel good, and they slap your hands. You got to really sneak around to smoke a reefer if yo' cramps is botherin' you. You got to smile when you don't want, and talk baby talk to get the guards to treat you right.

"You see, them guards out there are mostly men in women's bodies. They got the same kind o' cocksure ways as a pimp. Once in a while, you get a little soul from one of them, but most of them want to turn you into a slave as much as any man I ever met. You decide to act like you belong to yourself, and they crack down on you."

Juanita explained that she'd jumped bail in New Jersey. "You see, what happen, after servin' five years 'cause of Loose Larry's heroin habit, I finally get myself paroled for good behavior. Larry never once come to see me the whole five years I did fo' him. Not once. But as soon as he got wind I was out and workin' in New Jersey, he come 'round wantin' to claim me as one of his girls again. So one night he follows me home and tells me I still his chick, and then he holds a gun on me and knocks me down and fucks me hard. So I go wild and shoot him with his own gun, and that's how I end up in jail in Jersey. 'Cause I was over there workin' in a factory at the time. There I was, waitin' for a whole year to come to trial while they figurin' out how to appeal my case, and finally I get Johnny to bail me out if I work at his massage joint, but I get picked up again in a raid. So, here I am, honey. I expect a good long stay this time. After all, I did shoot him, even if he did fuck me over like a dog and mess up my whole life. I'm payin' for my sins, but if you have to pay for your sins to keep yo' soul, then that's sometimes the way it gotta be." Juanita finished her speech, and Dorissa could tell by her voice that she had slipped into a deep melancholy. "Let's light up this other reefer and get some sleep now," Juanita added.

Dorissa, after hearing Juanita's story, didn't have the heart to refuse her hospitality. They lit the marijuana and shared it in the darkness of the cell. Soon Dorissa drifted off, thinking how Oliver, Noah, and now Delila had gotten something of a hold on her soul.

Lie flat on your back on a hard surface. Slowly raise one knee and roll it over the other, until you are lying on your stomach. Allow the shoulders to follow through last. Now that you are on your stomach, slowly roll to your back again, leading with your shoulder. You should roll slowly around the floor, leg, hip, shoulder, following each other in a smooth and sensuous rhythm.

STEP 10:

The Rhythmic
Pelvic Thrust

"Are you crazy?" exclaimed Dorissa to Delila as she spoke through a plate-glass window in the visitors' room. "You expect me to stay in here for months so you can get an interesting trial going in the press?" She felt quite capable of resisting Delila's newest scheme. Seeing her on the other side of a plate-glass window made it easier to ignore her vivacious enthusiasm. "Delila, if you don't bail me out of here this minute, I'll never speak to you again! We'll have to find some other way to increase my notoriety. Because of your wild ideas, I might end up in jail for life!"

"I guess you're right. Now, in the light of day, it does seem like an extreme measure. I'd miss you too much! The judge set your bail at three thousand. It's a breeze. I'll have you out as soon as I can post the bond, snookums!" Delila gave in easily. This time Dorissa had been firm.

But before Delila could bail Dorissa out of Rikers Island,

Dorissa nearly caused a riot by teaching Juanita how to do the Rhythmic Pelvic Thrust during roof recreation time. Juanita, who had only survived because of her sense of levity, had managed to get the whole cellblock to join her in the dance.

Stand erect, legs slightly apart, knees a little flexed. Gently and smoothly, tilt the pelvis forward in a small thrusting motion. Relax and repeat.

When the dancer, emotionally exhausted from her week in the park and time in prison, arrived home that evening, she was greeted by the ringing telephone. First Oliver called to bombast her and inform her of his intention to sue for custody of Chrysta. Noah called to scold her and say, "I told you so." Her boss called to tell her she could never again return to teaching at St. Aloysius. Her day was complete.

Though her encounter with the indomitable Juanita Pietri and the inmates of Rikers Island's Women's House of Detention had inspired her to carry on her work for the Earth Mother, the sky was falling down around her ears. She was both thrilled and dismayed when Delila described the terrific amount of media coverage her performance and subsequent arrest had won. As she sat with the newspapers spread out before her, the phone rang once again. It was the talent agent, Pat Campley.

"Congratulations, dearie!" he chortled. "You have really learned your lesson about using the media for publicity. We're sure to get you a good line-up of gigs now!"

"What have I accomplished except to convince people that I'm a madwoman? I've been fired from my job, and I'm about to lose my child!" she howled at him. She felt alienated from everyone and had no intention of letting him suck her into any more of his party jobs. She terminated the conversation before he could explain himself any further. After sending Delila home so that she could have some contemplative solitude, Dorissa lay on the pillows under her Avocado Tree.

Unhappily, she imagined how rigidly Oliver would take charge of Chrysta. She dreaded never having wonderfully carefree days with the child again, watching the sunset, dancing together for the sheer joy of it. She remembered an afternoon a couple of weeks earlier when Chrysta smashed a fly on the windowpane and then recoiled in disgust when the yellow viscera oozed from it.

"It's life that's oozing from it. Life is wet and sticky and full of blood," Dorissa had explained to her. "Don't be afraid of it. Remember how I told you that women's bodies bleed every month because they have the power of growing life in them."

"Where will I be when I die? I'm scared to die!" Chrysta had suddenly expressed a classic fear, whimpering at the squashed fly.

"You'll be part of everything again. You'll be with Earth," Dorissa had answered, matter-of-factly. "Everything that you are made of has always been here on Earth, and you'll always be a part of it. You won't hurt when you're dead, but you're alive, and life knows nothing of death. Live bravely as though there is no death, and there will be none," she remembered telling the child as she hugged her close, twirling and whirling around the room, while the Avocado Tree smiled deep in its roots.

"Look at the pretty colors of the sunset!" Dorissa had shouted as they danced in the waxing light of the windows.

Now she felt of the Avocado Tree's leaves and remembered, once again, how she and Chrysta had planted the tree together. It had grown considerably since Dorissa had begun dancing for it. Its leaves spread out and over her, rich and full. She wished that Chrysta were there with her so that she could hold her in her arms, but Oliver was keeping her safe at his mother's house. Dorissa got up, watered the Tree, prayed to the Earth Mother that she would not lose Chrysta to Oliver, then fell fast asleep under its branches, dreaming she was dancing around the room with the child.

The next morning, on his way to the office, Noah arrived to visit, as if he were visiting a patient in a mental hospital.

"How are you feeling?" he asked gravely as he handed her a sympathetic bottle of Vitamin B Complex from the corner health-food store. He noted her disheveled appearance. She hadn't groomed or showered since her arrest. He searched her eyes for the hazy expression he was used to finding in his wife's.

"Not very well. Oliver has threatened to file suit for custody of Chrysta on grounds that I'm an unfit mother."

87

"Maybe you really ought to forget your dancing for a while to prove to Oliver that you are stable and can take care of the child," he said, taking her hand as if she were an invalid.

"But, don't you see, Noah, if I give up dancing, I'll be admitting instability. The only thing that will save me is going all the way with it and thumbing my nose at Oliver when I succeed. Otherwise everything that I've done and have been through will be in vain. Besides, I'll never get another job teaching, now. Fortunately, Pat Campley called and said that he's sure he can get me performances."

"Dorissa, you know what kind of performances he will get!" sighed Noah, reminding her of the Brand & Brand, Inc., fiasco in New Jersey.

"I've got to earn some money, somehow, or I won't be able to fight Oliver in court, and I'm not going to accept any more money from Delila. I'm already beholden to her for my bail. If I'm going to hang onto my soul, Noah, dancing is the only way!" She stomped into the kitchen, where she angrily poured herself a glass of orange juice.

He followed her and frowned gravely, taking all the wind out of her sails, just as Oliver used to. She wanted to throw her orange juice in his face, but instead she poured it down the front of her nightgown, sticking her tongue out at Noah and giving him a Bronx cheer.

"Don't be late for the office," she chided, mockingly handing him his briefcase.

She'd deliberately defied him, but all the same, after he left, she was crushed. She paced the floor, talking to her Avocado Tree. She began to doubt her own sanity and Delila's, too. Noah Levi-Museman had withdrawn his supportiveness, and she felt desperate without it. She remembered seeing a telephone number for a feminist psychotherapy referral service in *Majority Voice*. Maybe she really did need to get her head shrunk. An automatic answering service took her name and number and promised to call her back.

Soggy with orange juice, she fell down on her pillows amid her plants and wept bitterly. Once again she felt as absolutely hopeless as she had the afternoon over a year ago when she had been willing to meet her maker, head on, in the form of a *macho* Mack truck. The Avocado Tree silently endured her agony, as if it were all part of a necessary scheme. The phone rang, startling her.

"Hello, Ms. Femfunelli. This is Dr. Stone returning your call," said a cultured voice, not quite distinguishable as male or female.

"Oh yes," answered Dorissa, the referral service! She hoped that it was a voice of salvation.

"Well," said the sexually nebulus Dr. Stone, "what exactly is your problem?"

Dorissa had expected a woman to call back, so in her mind's eye she saw Dr. Stone as a woman. She'd had no experience with analysis, and so she decided that Dr. Stone wanted to hear, then and there, all that was troubling her psyche. She therefore proceeded to pour the mess of her life into the plastic mouthpiece of her push-button Touch-Tone phone, trying to tell all at once:

"Oh Doctor, everything's wrong. I'm thirty-four, and I was divorced last year; I have an eight-year-old child, and I was arrested for indecent exposure and assaulting an officer with my finger cymbal, and my ex-husband is trying to take my daughter away from me. No one understands that I was belly dancing for the return of Demeter, to balance the masculine urge with the feminine. Besides which, I've recently begun having an affair with another woman, because she makes me feel like an equal, but actually she's the reason I got arrested. She says she'll show me how to be a superstar, but all I want to do is redeem all the garbage, get more trees planted, stop plutonium waste and get the dog shit off the streets for the sake of the Earth Mother. . . ."

"Wait a minute, dahling! You're going too fast for me!" said Dr. Stone with a perfect Tallulah Bankhead delivery.

"Oh I'm sorry, Doctor, but you called when I was contemplating a Mack truck. . . ."

"Ms. Femfunelli, just tell me, how often do you masturbate?"

"Oh no, I can't believe you're asking me that! Are you a colleague of Narcissa Tittel, by any chance?" Dorissa became disheartened with Dr. Stone. Perhaps this was not the voice of salvation, after all.

"Never mind, dear. We don't have to talk about it right now if it causes you anxiety or discomfort to do so," answered Dr. Stone calmly.

"Ah," thought the discomforted, anxious Dorissa, "that's a fairly rational statement. I'd rather not talk about it right now."

"I simply feel that all problems of anxiety have a sexual basis. It's my psychotherapeutic technique! I suit the sex to the patient. Whatever you feel you want and need, Ms. Femfunelli," said Dr. Stone, beginning to sound more like a man than a woman.

"Is there something wrong with your voice, Doctor?" asked Dorissa, sheepishly.

"How is your sex life in general? Wouldn't you like to tell me all about it? Then I'll know whether you're the patient for me and I'm the doctor for you!"

"Well," Dorissa suspected that Dr. Stone was a man, after all, "you don't . . . I mean you aren't . . . one of those doctors I read about in *New York* magazine, who use sexual relations as part of the therapeutic approach with your patients . . . are you, Doctor?"

"Please, Ms. Femfunelli, if that were true, I certainly wouldn't tell you on the telephone. That would be unprofessional of me, wouldn't it?"

"Yes, I guess it would!" said Dorissa, a little exhausted by the mental gymnastics it took to be interviewed by Dr. Stone in order to find out if, indeed, she, or he, was the voice of salvation. In the midst of her tremendous suicidal depression, she stopped being able to make sense of anything.

"What exactly is your problem in narrower terms, Ms. Femfunelli?"

"I'm sitting here covered with orange juice and I called to find out what, exactly, my problem is. I don't have any money to fight my ex-husband's suit for custody of my daughter. He's a college professor, and he's suing on grounds that I'm unstable. Unless I can prove my seriousness as a belly dancer, or get famous enough to be taken seriously as an artist, no matter what I do, I'll just seem like a kook to the judge when I try to prove I'm a fit mother. I was fired from my teaching job for exposing myself in the park, so everything's against me. My agent says he can get me some jobs, but he's a far-out transvestite who wants me to teach him to belly dance, too! The difficulty is, how am I going to have enough money to prove my sanity, and what's more, *am I really sane?*" She began to tear at her hair.

"Now, Ms. Femfunelli, control yourself! Your only real problem is financial, and *have I got a job for you!* A wonderful job offer for a woman like you, came in just this morning from my colleague Dr. Gold. It's just professional embarrassment that keeps me from taking the job myself. It's terrific money! Five thousand dollars in one afternoon!"

"What?" Dorissa perked up a little. Five thousand dollars would hire a lawyer, or, at least, retain one.

"Do you have a pencil and paper handy? I'll give you all the specs."

Dorissa rummaged up a scrap of paper and a pencil. "Yes, go ahead."

"Call Dr. Gold at 699-6996. He has a patient who is looking for a woman to urinate in his mouth. He'll pay five thousand dollars!"

Dorissa began to feel a little faint. She wasn't at all sure she'd heard correctly.

"You choose the location, either your home or a hotel. You'll be paid either in cash or certified check, on the spot. You can have the money just before you do the job."

"What was the job, again, Doctor? I seem to have missed something." She leaned against the wall for support.

"You heard me all right, dahling! There's no need to pretend shock. You seem to get around!" reprimanded Doctor Stone with his Tallulah Bankhead voice. "This man is a wealthy businessman. He just needs to live out his erotic fantasy. Dr. Gold must know what he's doing for his patient! If this were some poor schnook who'd saved up all his life for this one thrill, I'd say, 'Don't do it,' but he can afford it and he knows what he's doing, and he's not hurting anyone. You're over eighteen, and it says here you can remain anonymous."

Dorissa was distraught enough to be intimidated by Dr. Stone's reasoning. Weakly, she verified the name and number. "Dr. Gold; 699-6996." The morality she'd learned as a bourgeois girl had proven itself to be a pile of bullshit. Neither morality nor sanity were absolutes, but depended on cultural definition. She'd had her credits in anthropology. Probably the ancient Zoobonese of Siberia urinated in each others' mouths as a religious rite. Sanity was as varied as the nerves of the universe, coursing energy through all creation. *Propriety was one thing, sanity another!*

In a fog, she pondered what Dr. Stone said as he continued. "Here are the specifications: You must wear a skirt just above the knee; lacey black garter belt and nylon stockings, but no panties. Your pubic hair must be shaved and you must squat directly over the gentleman's mouth, being careful not to get any urine on his chin. No words are to be exchanged. You are both to remain anonymous. Then take your five grand and go!"

"I feel like I've just been given an anesthesia! I feel numb all over!" said Dorissa, more weakly than ever.

"Well, dahling, you've got the name and number and all the specs! My guess is that your problem is basically financial!"

Dorissa placed her green, push-button Touch-Tone receiver back into its lucite cradle. She felt faint and wished she were a Sabine woman about to be carried off forever. She imagined her body gored by a bull.

But five thousand dollars. That was something to consider. This was America, where women's bosoms, factories for the milk of life, were plastered across billboards, selling everything from cigarettes to potato chips. Sex even sold pizza in America, and the Betty Crocker, Duncan Hines, boxed and powdered, instant upside-down cake was the dollar-sign pie in the sky.

The phone rang again, jangling her nerves.

"Hello, sweetheart; it's Delila. How do you feel?"

The question was all the encouragement Dorissa needed. She started to bawl, letting it all hang out. She poured the mess of her life into her green Touch-Tone, once again, topping it off with the cherry of Dr. Stone's incredible call.

"Well, sweetheart, five G's is Five G's, but forget it! I think you need a little rest and relaxation away from it all. I'll be over in an hour to whisk you away to the island for a quiet weekend of strategy planning. *We have to strike while the iron is hot!* That's what the fortune cookie I had with my Chinese breakfast said!" Delila cheerfully promised to be there in an hour.

Dorissa wasn't sure she wanted to become even more deeply involved with her, but if she wasn't going to have Delila's help to keep her rights to Chrysta, she was going to need to hire her own lawyer. She cradled her plastic receiver once again. Delila Dandi was driving over to whisk her away to luxury and superstardom, Noah Levi-Museman was about to call the men in the little white coats, and in her hand was a scrap of paper that burned a five-thousand-dollar sign into her retinas.

"To sell out, or not to sell out? That is the question!" she thought. Just then, there was an eager knock at the door. She peeked out the peepsight of her front door and saw Oliver standing in the hall. Forgetting how she looked, in her juicy nightgown and uncombed hair, she opened the door. Oliver stood before her in his neat lightweight summer suit and starched sport shirt. Beside him was a short, squat man in a navy-blue suit and tie.

"Dorissa, this gentleman has something for you. I thought it would be too inhuman to let him come alone with it." The man handed her a folded piece of paper. "See you in court, ma'am!" he said.

Dorissa took the paper and read "SUMMONS" on the front of it. The squat man turned on his heels and disappeared down the hall, as Oliver spoke firmly.

"Dorissa, I hope you're seeing a doctor, for your own good. Here are the names of a couple of psychiatrists my friends told me about."

Numbly, she took Oliver's piece of paper in hand.

"Take care of yourself," he said. She watched the back of his close-cropped head as he exited down the hall. For now, Delila Dandi was her only hope. She pulled an overnight bag from her closet and stuffed a few articles into it, along with the large jar of a Vitamin B Complex formula for stress that Noah had given her. The telephone sang out again.

"Hello, this is Dr. Albatrosky from The Feminist Psychotherapy Referral Service," said a woman's voice in a clipped and businesslike tone. "You called and left your name with our service earlier today. I'm returning your call."

"Yes, you already returned my call," said Dorissa, indignantly describing her conversation with Dr. Stone.

93

"What?" said the voice with surprise. "There's no Dr. Stone with our service! Some crank caller must have phoned our number and got your message and really pulled the wool over your eyes. I must apologize for the inconvenience. Please be assured that everything will be done to trace down the source of this annoyance call," said Dr. Albatrosky in a clear and efficient tone. "But Ms. Femfunelli, never discuss your sex life over the telephone with strangers! *It's not rational!*"

STEP 11:

The Wind-swept Tree Sway

As Delila, in her private speedboat, chauffered Dorissa across the blue waters of Long Island's Great South Bay toward Cherry Grove, Delila explained that the infamous community had been founded by gay postwar veterans in the thirties. Along the resort beaches of Fire Island, some of the most beautiful and well-groomed men in the world sunned themselves, lying in languid poses that invited each other to oral or anal pleasures.

"It's Sodom and Gomorrah!" exclaimed Dorissa as Delila led her like a camel by the nose through clumps of bronzing bodies lolling on sandy dunes and beaches.

"No, it's the birth of the Great Androgyne!" protested Delila, laughing at Dorissa's bewilderment. "A great twentieth-century French sociologist predicted that humanity would become woman and man, love and thought, tenderness and strength, grace and energy!"

In the aesthetic setting where white sand sloped down to a pounding sea, Dorissa noticed that people looked at each other as neither one sex nor another. Gay men and women ogled the bikini-clad Dorissa as she passed with the tanned and topless Delila snuggling at her side.

"Let's kiss and amuse the boys!" teased Delila as she swept Dorissa into her arms and they stood, ankle-deep in surf, sun beating down on their curvaceous bodies. "You must learn how to relax and accept the pleasures of it all, Little Isis!"

Delila was a sort of female Hugh Hefner, but with more soul. She was purely sensual and a romantic who could sigh as much over the taste of a peach as her lover's lips. She could be as ecstatic over the delicate smell of a woman or the feel of a woman's satin skin as she could over the pungent aroma of a man or his brawny, hairy chest. Dorissa found that Delila awakened in her a tactile appreciation for the voluptuous Earth. Dorissa sighed over sunsets, petted peaches, and crunched into apples with a greater intensity than ever before.

Still, the culture shock provided by Cherry Grove, Fire Island, was more than Dorissa could comfortably endure. It was a fantasy world that tinseled more than it shined, a world with no immortality in its eggs or seeds, sperm or ova. "If only Delila were a man," thought Dorissa, "I'd really flip over her. Why can't Noah take my dancing as seriously as she does? Why aren't I as free to be myself with him?" She felt exhausted by the subtle difference in status between herself and men, tired of trying to please them and satisfy their dominating egos. Delila was teaching her the potency of the female psyche. Dorissa began to feel self-possessed as Delila inspired in her a new courage to go ahead with her dancing despite Oliver's and now Noah's disapproval.

"The time is exactly ripe for you to make a huge splash, a tremendous flash in the pan of success!" declared Delila as they sipped iced drinks on the sun deck of her Fire Island estate. As an expert sociologist turned successful businesswoman, there was no doubt that she knew whereof she spoke.

"Female strength," responded Dorissa, launching into poetic revery, "is in the abdomen, meant for housing and giving birth, not in the deadly, weapon-wielding bicep! If I'm going to get anywhere at all, I'm going to continue to lead with my belly until they understand!"

As the lights across the quiet bay began to dot the shore and the coppery sun dipped into the water to cool itself, then sank beyond the curve, Delila murmured of love to Dorissa.

"Love, my dear Little Isis, is understanding another's feelings. And who can understand your feelings more than another woman, like myself? Hasn't the literature of men been one long everlasting complaint about the insoluble mystery of woman? Aren't we the only ones who know that there is no mystery at all, only an emptiness longing to be filled with love?" She gripped Dorissa's hand. If she was going to fulfill her fantasy of creating a superstar, she knew she had to keep Dorissa's trust. "Perk up, dahling, you'll show them yet!"

Delila was as reassuring to Dorissa as a mother hen. By the time they arrived back in the city on Monday morning, Delila's charisma had restored Dorissa's flagging confidence. Delila had convinced her that the media coverage she'd received was all to the good.

"Look, dahling," she explained, "my lawyers are going to stall off the hearing until you've made a big enough splash to have a good bargaining position. If you play your cards right, you'll be a superstar before you come to trial, and then you can't lose custody of Chrysta. Americans think that anyone who is famous and makes a lot of money is *sane*."

"But Delila," protested Dorissa, "I just want to be taken seriously as a ritual dancer for women and the Earth! I don't care how famous or rich I get so long as I can keep Chrysta and dance." She stroked the leaves of her Avocado Tree as she watered it.

Delila's plan was to join forces with Pat Campley, whom Dorissa had told her about. She would use his office as a front to launch a big promotional scheme for the dancer. She planned to wine and dine Campley at an exclusive restaurant on the Upper East Side before he had a chance to contact Dorissa again and tempt her into performing for him.

Dorissa and Delila glided tanned and sunglassed into Les Goulet and surveyed the people lunching in the dining room. Dorissa didn't see Pat Campley anywhere. Finally she spied a gray-blond, blue-eyed, cheek-blushed, and eye-linered woman sitting at a table in the corner and realized that she was contemplating Mr. Campley's smile on the woman's face. He'd shown up dressed as a Ms.

"There he is!" gulped Dorissa.

"Oh my," laughed Delila. "He looks exactly like a woman. It's hysterical! How utterly amusing. I'd never have guessed he was a man if I sat across from him all night. Hmmmm, he's adorable!"

"Hi girls! What a cute pant-suit you've got there!" Pat Campley complimented Delila as she slid into the plush seat alongside him.

"Yours is adorable, too, dahling!" Delila returned the compliment, snuggling up to him.

"Oh, your friend really sends me," said Pat to Dorissa. "I hope you don't mind my dressing up, girls!" he prattled. "I just couldn't resist when I knew I'd be dining with two women. I couldn't bear to show up all drab and masculine when I knew you two would be gorgeous and tan after your weekend on the Island."

Delila and Pat hit it off immediately. They were both businessmen in women's clothing, and both agreed that Dorissa should follow up her Battery Park escapade with another media-baiting performance, before America's one-eyed monsters could forget they'd held her in the screens of their pupils, before another moment of prime time was wasted!

"Look," said Delila, leaning over soufflé to talk turkey, "I've got my lawyers working on a civil liberties suit for sex discrimination. There were at least twenty bare-breasted men in that park last Monday, and not one of them was arrested for indecent exposure! My strategy ought to be good for a few more news items on the media, and especially in the women's lib papers."

"You are a woman after my own heart," swooned Pat, looking deep into Delila's brown eyes.

Dorissa surveyed her luxuriant surroundings. She had decided to listen to what they said and use it for her own plan, but she became acutely aware of the solicitous service the waiters were providing the well-dressed and perfumed clientele of the rich mahogany-lined and green-ferned dining room. She poked at her soufflé with the prongs of her fork. The thought that came to her as its puffy crown began collapsing was a self-tortured one.

"Here I am," she mused, "while millions are starving for a crust of bread, or being tortured because of the avarice of some madman—decadently slurping watercress soup and unpuffing soufflé; ugh!"

Self-torturing thoughts always seemed to come to her at moments that offered the most supreme of pleasures. Suddenly, for the first time in her life, she was aware of their hidden meaning. They represented her need to punish herself, to feel undeserving, as though the experience of pleasure was too painful to endure. She remembered the thoughts of horror that used to come to her during the lust of conjugal love. Images of herself being tortured, or dying in a fire from which there was no escape, flooded her mind without invitation. Into the foreplay of orgasmic release came the faces of starving children, pictures of torture victims, thoughts of electrical shock devices used on the genitals of political insurgents, leering faces of hangmen, firing squads, rapists, screams of agony distorting human expressions with deforming animal howls. These images concentrated their grip on her as she tried to be free of them and surge toward orgasm. Only by fighting them out of her mind could she let the burning, cooling waves of fire and ice sweep over her.

Now, for the first time, as she sat between Delila and Pat, two people who had totally came to grips with themselves, she understood the guilt woven into her psyche. The Avocado Tree sent out a subliminal long-distance message. "You've suffered the world's guilt in order to be called! Now let it fall away, priestess. Do your thing!" it iterated through the psychic plasma of her brain, assembling thoughts in her head like the voice of Billie Burke. She awoke to the conversation bouncing back and forth between her two "female" companions. They were batting her destiny back and forth like a volley ball. Suddenly she found her tongue dancing as eloquently as her belly.

"Think of those early priestesses of the Earth Mother who first belly danced, rolling their bellies in the name of fertility!" She was startled to hear her voice come out with such firm authority,

99

just as she'd been surprised to handle the newsmen who thrust microphones in her face in Battery Park.

Having interrupted the business conversation, she continued: "What a sense of body freedom those ancient women must have felt! They had no doubts they were doing the right thing! Dancing to populate the Earth and work her soil for food. More and more life had to be brought forth to combat death. Mother Nature was law, and birth and death her most primal mysteries! Women didn't need to feel like guilty Pandoras or Eves. They felt like robust fertility goddesses, not temptresses!"

Pat and Delila exchanged shrugs as Dorissa continued quite animatedly: "If woman is going to regain her status as divine life-giver, she is going to have to fuck guilt! I'm going to start enjoying myself and the luxuriant fruits of Earth right now!" She plunged into her soufflé, brought a forkful of it to her mouth, and devoured it in one salivating gulp. "Ummmmm," she remarked, "good!"

"Are you all right, dahling?" asked Delila, amazed by Dorissa's peculiar outburst. Delila was beginning to worry that her Trilby's spiritual fervor was turning into a raging fever. "We're talking *percentages* and you're talking *primal mysteries!* Are you with us, dear?"

"Oh I think the priestess is adorable when she pops off like that," interjected Pat. "Don't you see, Deli'? That's why we can package her so easily. *She's for real!* An honest-to-goddess priestess of the clit! She tickles the hell out of me! I hope to worship at her vulval shrine someday!"

Dorissa was lost in her own reverie. "Don't you understand, Delila? This is more than packages and percentages! We have got to replace every horrifying act of man's bloody weaponry with a groan of woman's pleasure! Men are struggling to be free of Earth's belly! They build fiery phalluses to fly over her thighs and explode bombs in the faces of children. Men are the mercenary soldiers of wars. My friend Juanita Pietri is right! Let Hitler sodomize Stalin in hell, let them shoot their violent adolescent mother hostilities and murderous rebellions up each other's asses! I've had it with this intellectual, patriarchal guilt trip. My *belly* is my medium! I feel like dancing!" Dorissa stood up.

100

"Not now, dahling, please, calm down," said Delila, pulling her down and casting a sidelong glance at Pat. "Hand me that glass of chablis she's been sipping. You didn't drop any acid in it, did you, Betty Boop?"

"She's farther out every time I see her! She's better than Billy Graham! *Sheer dynamite!* We'll have her on "The Marv Gavett Show" before the year is out!" chortled Pat, clapping his hands together and giggling wildly.

"I hope you're right! What exactly is our very next move?" asked Delila, anxious to bring the conversation back to business.

"I've got just the thing!" exclaimed Pat. "There's a mammoth rock festival going on this weekend in Woodstock. There will be plenty of television and news reporters around, and we can expose her to the under-thirty crowd. My friend is one of the producers. If the kids dig her, we'll be *in*. They're the biggest fad market going. My producer chum is a far-out body painter, and he wants to body-paint the priestess and have her dance nude at the festival. We can cash in on the media coverage as well as cook up a little of our own!"

"It's perfect for a follow-up to Battery Park!" laughed Delila, thrilling Pat by squeezing his panty-hosed knee. "I like you, Patty; we think alike! This girl will be a star property in a month if we keep our little heads together. She'll be the biggest flash in the pan this society has ever seen!"

Dorissa didn't like being a pawn in Delila's and Pat's fast-talking chess game. Dorissa pricked her soufflé again, watching its yellow belly sink all the way down. She knew what her own motives were, but she was silent for now. Instinctively, she'd decided to go along and see where these two media moguls would take her. Even if Delila's and Pat's scheme backfired, she needed Delila's lawyers to defend her custody of Chrysta, and she needed to stall for time.

That evening, as she lay beneath her Avocado Tree enjoying a little solitude, a sense of peace invaded Dorissa's body, and she slept soundly for the first time since her arrest. She dreamed that her arms and hands were branches and leaves, and she floated through the air of her apartment in a *pas de deux* with her Avocado Tree.

Move to your own music. Let your fingers ripple, let your body sway, like trees in the wind. Lift your arms to the sky. Know that you're alive in the moment, in the flesh, your own reason for dancing. Let the swirling energy flow through your legs and arms. Move in tune with the rhythm of the universe.

· STEP 12:

The Leaf Shimmy

A few days later, Dorissa arrived in Woodstock, an antique artists' community nestled in the Lower Catskills of New York State. Delila and Pat stayed in New York City to hustle the media at its center. Pat's friend, the body painter Chin Lo Slung, met Dorissa at the bus. He was a handsome, smooth-skinned, tawny, and muscular fellow wearing tight black denims. His long, pitch-black hair, braided in an oriental queue, hung down his shirtless back. He wore a tiny red mandarin vest.

"I've seen lots of publicity all over town about your dance. Old Patty's been working hard, really doing a job of it! There's a big powwow going on this evening at the festival grounds," Chin informed Dorissa. "An Iroquois Indian medicine man from the Mohawk Reservation by the name of Bill Schenectady has been advertising all week, too. He's coming down from the mountains to make a prophecy and sing tribal songs."

Chin Lo Slung drove Dorissa to his studio in the mountains. An hour later she lay nude, entirely covered in dayglow multicolored green body paint, as Chin carefully dipped his brush into his pallet to finish the last green leaf, which curled around her navel. He'd used a motif of ferns and heart-shaped philodendron leaves.

"Okay, that's it! You're done, baby, and you look great!"

Dorissa felt very relaxed and ready to perform. Chin had given her an acupressure massage to help her lie perfectly still as he worked. He knew how to make his human canvases enjoy their body work. The little tickles of his brush had hypnotized Dorissa's muscles into total relaxation. His exquisitely rococo painting enhanced the curves of her body with swirling leaves.

"Well, I'm ready. Let's get the show on the road before I get smeared!" laughed Dorissa, contemplating her green navel as the source of several leafy vines.

She arrived at the rock festival grounds in Chin's baroquely painted Volkswagen bus. She was due to perform as soon as the Indian chief finished his prophecy. Chin explained that the medicine man, Bill Schenectady, had been expected in Woodstock for weeks. "He says he's come to deliver a prophecy. After that, he plans to go back to the reservation for his dance rituals and never leave his people again. Everyone's been talking about The New Age, the Apocalypse, and American destiny. The kids are all excited about his message.

Chin led Dorissa, covered with a light robe to conceal her body paint, through herds of blue-jeaned young people stretched out over the land for what seemed like a mile. Bill Schenectady, Iroquois medicine man, was on the platform with some of his Indian followers. He wore an open blue denim work shirt, blue jeans, suede leather vest with fringes, and western cowboy boots. His red-brown skin angled up over his face bones. His straight, dark hair, was banded in place by feathered leather. He wore sunglasses and talked in phrases filled with images of eagles. Intense and sincere, his strong presence was everything one would expect from a spiritual adviser to AIM, and a veteran of Wounded Knee. He wielded his microphone like Mick Jagger as he spoke his prophecy:

"Over a hundred years ago my people prophesied that there would be a lighted box that would show news events, that there would be long trailways in the sky and giant machines, like eagles with metal wings, that would fly. They said that many species of animals would be dying. Then, they said, there would be floods, earthquakes, blizzards, and famines, as if the Earth were revolting against inhumanity."

Dorissa nearly flipped out as she listened to Bill Schenectady. Here was everything her Avocado Tree had been teaching her, subliminally, for' weeks. It surfaced in her consciousness like Venus rising from the sea. She was ecstatic as she pushed her way closer to the stage to get a better view of the Indian. Chin Lo Slung trailed after her as she stepped gingerly over the blue-jeaned legs and denim-shirted bodies sprawled around the grassy slope.

The impressive medicine man continued in his somber voice: "Pray for the Earth," he pleaded, pointing to the ground in front of the stage. "Put your heart in the Earth. The Earth is wounded and is soon to give birth. She needs your prayers because she's having a hard time. She's all we've got, brothers and sisters. You don't need an alien guru! We, the Indians, *native* to this land, have the truth of this land, your America! We are the roots here!" He pointed to his heart. "We know the truth. If you love this Earth, you'll make it through. It may be rough, a bloodbath, a terrible apocalypse!" He opened his hands and raised them above his head. "Something is going to happen here, in *this* land, first!"

Dorissa fell to her knees on the grass as if she were about to go into her birth mime. She expostulated a huge sigh, making Chin Lo Slung worry that she might smear her body paint.

Many blue-jeaned people in the crowd yelled, "Right on, baby!" as the medicine man's tone became increasingly ominous:

"The Earth, Our Mother, is going to reclaim all that is Hers. She will revolt against the unnatural. A great war will be upon us, as people everywhere fight for food, and the Earth sends up wind storms, tidal waves, blizzards, famine, drought, and purifying fires! The Earth is everything. Love Earth. Pray for her. *Touch a tree!* Pray for all living things!"

"Touch a tree and pray for *Her*." Dorissa whispered intently. Chin was now grooving on her ecstasy as she knelt and sighed. Her hands clutched together under her chin, she looked like a child saying her bedtime prayers.

Bill Schenectady signaled his followers, and as they chanted and played tom-toms and shakers, he concluded, his voice booming from the amplifiers: "Go out and do the work of the day, dance a ritual, refresh your prayers to the Earth with every bite of food or thing you do. Just like my people, learn the old ways, again. Learn the wild edibles, how to fish and hunt food for yourselves! Unfreeze the Earth packaged in your cans and refrigerators and *plant gardens!*"

"Okay, baby, you're next!" said Chin to Dorissa. "Give it all you got!" But he might as well have saved his breath, because Dorissa, feeling complete rapport with the Indian's message, doffed her robe, donned her finger cymbals, and danced wildly toward the stage. When she reached it, she improvised a belly dancing *pas de deux* with the medicine man who had begun to stomp in rhythm with the tom-toms and shakers. Their psychic plasma was immediately in tune. Body paint and dance rituals were right up Bill Schenectady's alley. The lighting technicians hit the stage with strobes, and Bill Schenectady, in the flashing light, looked as if he were dancing with a female tree. The blue-jeaned and denimed crowd went wild as Dorissa rolled her belly and bumped her hips at the Indian. Bill Schenectady enjoyed himself too. After all, he'd graduated from Yale and was no slouch. His leather fringes tickled her posterior as deftly as Chin's paintbrush. When Dorissa's own taped music boomed from the amplifiers, she took over the microphone. She sensed that she had won the raving crowd, which was ready to receive her feminine message about Mother Earth and ritual worship. She belly danced like a naked stalk of iridescent vegetation, and the huge, youthful crowd watched enthralled. She felt as though she'd been to the mountaintop. Nothing could stop her now, not even Oliver!

The next morning, before she left Woodstock, Noah called to congratulate her and tell her that her nude dance, on the eleven-o'clock news, was quite artful. "On my TV screen, you looked just like an illustration of the 'Lady of the Plants,' which I found in Neumann's Jungian book *The Great Mother!*" he exclaimed, sure that his pronouncement thrilled her. He was trying to make up to her for his negative attitude the week before. Delila and Pat called next to say that she would be on the cover of the *Village*

Vocalizer, a widely circulated underground newspaper read especially by the under-thirty generation.

The vigor of her triumph the evening before made her bound, like a deer, into Chin's baroquely painted Volkswagen bus for the ride back to New York. Chin drove by the festival grounds to pick up his chief sound engineer, who was also returning to the city. As they stopped by the site of last night's prophetic performance, Dorissa was dismayed to note that the peace generation of Woodstock had left many empty Coke bottles and beer cans littering the grassy slope—scathing reminders that her Earth worship message had not penetrated dreamy young souls with ecological morality or respect for Mother Nature. She felt called to inspire them to personal action as she watched Chin reappear. He walked toward her across the littered field, accompanied by a tall denim-suited fellow sporting a bevy of gray-brown curls. When they entered the Volkswagen, Dorissa noted that the fellow was quite attractive in a mature, manly sort of way. He was slightly balding at the temples and had dark, satanic eyebrows, which arched higher as he spoke. He slid into the front seat alongside Dorissa. The side of his thigh pressed against the side of hers. Chin entered the driver's seat, started the bus, and introduced the curly-haired fellow as Stanislaus Yeski, chief sound engineer for the festival.

Stanislaus Yeski looked directly into her eyes and raised one satanic eyebrow. "After you make the front page of the *Times*, then what?" he asked sardonically.

Dorissa noticed that his face had the alchemy of an interesting personality. The lines around his eyes seemed etched by a special brand of awareness. She felt intimidated by his question and felt the need to explain where she was really at, just in case he was thinking that she was a mere ambitious entertainer, like the rock stars he'd usually dealt with. As they drove down the winding mountainside road, she launched into an explanation of her spiritual motives for the dance celebrating women and the Earth. He smiled directly into her eyes as if to say, "I know exactly where you're at, even better than you do."

When finally she paused, he retorted flatly: "I know you're a feminist belly dancer for Isis, but your jaw is too tight and your neck is too stiff. That's why your back aches a little, and I also can

107

see that you're beginning to get motion sickness from not breathing deeply enough."

Without seeming sexually aggressive, but with great authority, Stanislaus Yeski began to massage the back of Dorissa's neck. His expert fingers pressed deep into two very sensitive areas just beneath her medulla oblongata, sending tiny thrills of relaxation along her spine. "Look straight ahead and relax your jaw," he commanded gently.

"How did you know I was getting motion sickness?" she replied in a mumble, feeling incapable of resisting his help.

"I could tell by looking at you. I read bodies," he explained. "Your back is hyperflexed. So are your knees. I watched you dancing. Your posture is what gave you a big ass and large thighs. And your posture has been sociologically induced by a repressive moral ethic that makes women into *passive* sex objects."

Dorissa did not appreciate his familiarity with her anatomy, but his neck massage was too good to refuse.

"I've been in Reichian therapy for ten years," he continued. "I've worked on my body, especially breathing. My asthma was cured by it. Correct breathing depends on good posture; posture on sociological conditioning. Women in our culture usually stand the way you do, with hyperflexed knees and weight tilted backward toward the heel—with their asses out—a classic pin-up pose that makes it easy for them to be pinned down. It makes them literal pushovers for masculine domination, makes it easy for them to be knocked down and knocked up, harder for them to say 'No'!"

Dorissa was fascinated. So that was why she'd always had such trouble saying "No." She cleared her throat.

"See, your throat is loosening up. It means you're beginning to breathe better," he was quick to observe. "How do you feel?"

"Much better, thanks," she admitted, settling back in the seat to look again at Stanislaus, whose face seemed less satanic and more angelic now.

"Reich is one of my heroes," he sighed. "Reichian theory should be an interesting subject for a belly dancer. Why don't you join me at my studio when we get to the city?" He looked sincerely into her eyes. "I'll give you a complete Reichian massage, and you can try out my orgone accumulator."

"Your orgone accumulator?" queried Dorissa, wide-eyed.

"Have you read about Kirlian photography of the human aura?"

"No, but I read about Kirlian photography and photosynthesis, when I was helping my former husband write his doctoral thesis in biology."

"Well, it proves that Reich's orgone box wasn't so far out after all. The human aura is the electromagnetic charge, the biochemical energy he was talking about. I built an orgone accumulator in the shape of a pyramid. Your belly dance isn't the only thing those ancient Egyptians had right. I think Reich should have used a pyramid instead of a box. My accumulator really charges you up! You've got to try it. My ex-wife was a famous rock singer, and she had me recharge her before every performance. It worked like a charm to increase her aura."

Dorissa sat fascinated as Stanislaus continued. Chin every now and then added his own theories to the conversation, explaining how acupuncture charts of the human nervous system augmented what Stanislaus said.

"That chick you were married to used you good, man!" he empathized with Stanislaus, who seemed to avoid the subject of his ex-wife in favor of expounding his theories to Dorissa.

"I'm really into the biophysics of sound. Just picture yourself in a fish tank hearing the waves and ripples in the water as they touch and caress your body!" Stanislaus once again caressed Dorissa's neck. "Relax; you're letting your neck tighten up again," he gently commanded as her motion sickness momentarily threatened to return.

Upon arriving in New York, Dorissa found herself whisked in a taxi to a sound studio located on a side street in Greenwich Village. She called Delila's answering service to leave a telephone number where she could be reached. Before long, she was listening to Mozart's *G-Minor Symphony* by means of the most incredible sound system she'd ever seen. Speakers were placed around a huge white room in every conceivable position. They were the only furnishings in the room, except for a purple velvet-covered water bed, rocking gently as a boat. She occupied the center of it. Speakers shaped like cones, like boxes, like Henry Moore sculptures with amorphous limbs, surrounded her.

"You see, the sound waves are constantly hitting your body and passing through you from every direction," explained Stanislaus with a satisfied gleam in his eyes. "This way, your whole body listens to the music, and every possible inch and angle of it is hit by waves of vibrations bouncing off your skin and traveling through your organs. You get to hear the way a fish in a tank of water hears."

"Yes," murmured Dorissa, lost in a sensuous rapture of sound. Before long she found herself lying naked, except for her orange bikini panties, in a pyramid-shaped orgone accumulator.

Stanislaus Yeski's hands reached in through holes in the sides of the pyramid to massage her neck, back, and belly.

"Stan," she protested mildly, "isn't this getting a little too personal?"

"You are having sexual *feelings*," he said, "but you don't have to act upon them or do anything about them. Just flow with it. Learn to let your feelings go. Only think about controlling your *actions*, not your feelings. *They're very healthy*. That's the first step toward learning to breathe properly and easily."

"Oh," said Dorissa, not totally sure of what Stan said, but noticing he'd begun to strip down to his underwear.

"Maybe you'll feel less threatened if I take off my clothes, too," he said in his logical tone. Dorissa was aware that as he continued to massage her belly and thighs, the front of his blue bikini shorts bulged more and more. She expected that any minute he would approach her with more than his hands, but he didn't. She almost began to want him to when the phone rang, relieving her of the anxiety of decision.

"You'd better answer the phone, Stan!" she suggested.

"No need, my answering machine will do it!" he insisted as he massaged the middle of her forehead. "This is the area the psychics call 'the third eye.' Reich said it's an erogenous zone. It's highly concentrated with what the Russians call 'psychic plasma.'"

Dorissa had no way of knowing that at the moment, Delila was listening to the recorded message with which Stanislaus answered his telephone.

"Ahh (sigh, groan, sigh, grunt), ummmm," spoke Stanislaus' voice into Delila's ear. "This is Stanislaus Yeski Sound Studios. Please leave your name and number after the orgasmic groan. "There was a magnificent groan and a beep to punctuate the message.

Delila was at once disturbed. What was this sound studio, and who was this character her Trilby dared to visit without her? Livid with jealousy, she rustled the pages of the Manhattan directory and found an address for Yeski Studios. Then she leaped into her red Mercedes, like Sir Lancelot onto his charger, and was off.

Before Stanislaus could answer the studio buzzer, Delila Dandi, her eyes afire with apprehension, burst into the back room. She'd heard Dorissa grunting, groaning, and sighing in agony and ecstacy as Stanislaus worked out one knotted muscle and then another. Unable to contain herself, Delila flew into the room and discovered Dorissa lying in the strange orgone pyramid, which to her adrenaline-driven mind looked like a madman's torture device. Stanislaus' hands were inserted into the holes on one side. Dorissa's head, blindfolded to keep out disturbing light, was visible through another side.

"Let go of her, you maniac!" shouted Delila in her most threatening tone. Quicker than the unsuspecting masseur, she bounded across the room, swung her huge pocketbook with all her might, and felled him, in one fell swoop, like a knight a dragon.

"Ahhhh (sigh), (groan), ummmm," he moaned as he lay prostrate and unconscious on the floor of his studio under the amorphous limbs of one of his speakers.

Dorissa removed her blindfold just in time to see Stanislaus bite the dust. "Delila, what have you done?" she cried.

"What do you mean, 'what have you done?'" Delila was aghast. "I've just saved you from the jaws of this dragon!"

"No, Delila dear, this is no dragon. This," she explained, kneeling over Stanislaus, patting him on the cheeks, "is Stanislaus Yeski, professional sound engineer and amateur Reichian therapist. My God, I hope he isn't dead!" she added when he didn't respond to her ministrations.

"Of course he's not dead, silly," answered Delila, annoyed at Dorissa's seeming lack of gratitude for her heroic rescue. "He's merely stunned! What's that torture contraption?"

"That," answered Dorissa, with growing concern for Stan's condition, "is an orgone pyramid, built by this very clever fellow you've just done in with your pocketbook."

"Oh dear," thought Delila, "my pocketbook! I forgot I was carrying a little present in there for you! A miniature in marble of Rodin's 'Isadora Duncan'! See!" She pulled the sculpture from her pocketbook and held it out to Dorissa. "I bought it to celebrate the anniversary of our meeting and your triumph in Woodstock! I hope it's not broken!"

"Probably not," groaned Dorissa, "but I bet poor Stan's head is!"

"Why are you so worried about that blackguard, anyway?" Delila grew more annoyed and uncomprehending. "What was he doing to you in that contraption?"

"Delila dear, that, as I've said, is merely an orgone pyramid, and Stan here was simply giving me an energizing Reichian massage, combined with acupressure technique, with some Edgar Cayce massage oil. His hands are absolutely angelic, and now, I think, you've killed him."

"No I haven't, I can't have," gasped Delila, beginning to get a little worried. "Here, let me see." She bent down over Stan and, placing her head to his chest, listened for a heartbeat. Her long hair tickled his face, bringing him half awake. Unconscious of what he was doing, he pulled his penis out of his bikini underwear and began massaging it with his still-oily hands.

"He's not dead, dear," said Delila, sardonically rolling her eyes to indicate Stanislaus' activity.

"What shall we do for him, Delila? Look at the nasty bruise that's beginning to show on his forehead!"

"Dahling, I don't think he needs us to do anything for him," retorted Delila. "He seems to be quite capable of taking care of himself! But if you insist, we can lift him over to that water bed and give him an ice pack!" She grabbed Stan's ankles, and Dorissa, with some struggle, lifted his shoulders. Dorissa and her Lancelot dragged the tall, felled, cock-in-hand dragon to his floating haven.

Waking up to the sight of Dorissa and Delila bending down over him as he lay on his water bed, Stanislaus thought he'd arrived in paradise. "Hmmmm," he moaned softly, "where am I?"

"You're right here at home, poor Stan, on your own water bed," cooed Dorissa.

"Ohhhh, I feel like I've been hit with a brick," he groaned.

"Not a cheap brick, dear; a marble copy of a Rodin!" Delila was still not convinced by Dorissa's explanation. "What kind of torture contraption is that?"

"Oh?" realized Stanislaus, "you're the maniac who hit me!"

"No, Stan; Delila's no maniac. She's a sociologist, a successful businesswoman, and my very closest friend."

"A sociologist! Christ, she must have read a lot about the Spanish Inquisition, or she's got an overactive imagination!" growled Stanislaus, holding his head.

"Now, *that* I'll admit to," said Delila. "My second analyst said I overfantasize."

"Look, I'm really sorry, Stan. Delila didn't mean to clobber you. She just acted impulsively," apologized Dorissa.

"Well, whatever she did, my head is killing me!"

Dorissa tried to soothe his forehead. "Oh dear, what can we do to make you feel better?"

"Well," he grinned impishly, a light dawning like a sunrise of sensuality in his eyes, "you can both give me a massage in my orgone pyramid to re-energize me.

"You seem to have quite a spark left in you," laughed Delila.

"Well, after all, you did knock me out cold, and for no reason." Stanislaus was as logical as ever.

"Well, all right," decided Delila, "you've asked for it. But watch out! My names not *Delila* for nothing!"

Stanislaus Yeski, pure sound and body sensualist incarnate, quietly stripped off his undershorts, stopping briefly to try to understand how his oily cock got outside of them. Then climbing a bit shakily into his orgone accumulator, he said, "Okay, women! I'm ready."

Delila, with some coaching from her cohorts, began to massage the orgone expert, adding a few techniques of her own in the genital area.

"Ahhhh, sheer energy! Pure frequency vibrations!" remarked Stanislaus every now and then as he submitted himself to the four soft hands of the two attractive women. It was not long before he was quite re-energized, and Delila, pure sensual adventuress incarnate, insisted on trying out the orgone pyramid, too. She quickly removed her clothes and hopped into the pyramid to allow Dorissa and Stanislaus to massage her. As all her biophysical energy became easily concentrated in her groin, rockets went up, cannons roared, firecrackers exploded, waves crashed on shores, horns blared, planes took off and landed, silos unloaded their grain, and flowers flew open spreading pollen as butterflies hatched from cocoons.

Stand erect, with knees slightly flexed and feet firmly on the floor. By tightening the knees in extremely rapid alternation, shake the abdomen and buttocks in a jiggling motion. The belly and buttocks must be relaxed so the Leaf Shimmy can occur. Learning to let it all hang out really helps!

As Delila's energy level climaxed in multiple sighs and moans of pleasure, Stanislaus exclaimed. "Wow, talk about orgastic potency! If Reich had known her, he'd have thrown his orgone box out the window!"

"Yes, Stan," Dorissa smiled proudly. "Delila is a totally liberated woman!"

STEP 13:

The Double Hip-bump

The most exciting result of Dorissa's Woodstock caper was an invitation, arriving through Pat Campley's office, to perform for the National Organization for Women. The prospect overwhelmed her. It was her dream come true. Pat Campley had recently contacted Rosalie Steinbauer, a leader of the feminist movement.

"You mean you know Rosalie Steinbauer? The leader of the Movement?" asked Dorissa incredulously of her talent agent as she sat across from him in his vaudeville-style office the next morning. She was impressed.

Pat Campley's blue eyes sparkled mischievously. "See what the right publicity can do, priestess? Rosalie and I get along fine!"

"*Mamma mia*, I'll be launched in the Movement!" She jumped up excitedly and gave Pat a kiss on his forehead. "The Movement!" She danced a little around the desk.

"Dorissa, honey, as a lesbianic transvestite I hope to find some measure of acceptance in the women's movement, too, because

I'm a lover of *all* that is female." Pat Campley gave Dorissa a girl-friendly hug as she left his office.

Later, as she lay under her Avocado Tree, dreaming of recent events in her life, Dorissa could hardly contain herself. She was to dance at the National Conference of NOW in Atlantic City. It was to be called the "Ms. America Pageant" and be staged directly across from the "Miss America Pageant." Rosalie Steinbauer's idea was to hire Dorissa to upstage the famous beauty queen and grab all the media coverage she could for her feminist cause.

Pat, with Delila's help, had convinced Rosalie that the best way to get media action for her conference was to stage Dorissa's belly dance to coincide with the Miss America Pageant. At the exact moment that Bert Parks crowned the "Miss It" of middle-class values—whose All-American smile made her just right for waving from a football float, whose breasts were too small to qualify her for *Playboy* and too large to qualify her for *Vogue*—Dorissa Femfunelli would bare her notorious belly.

The big convention was more than a month away, in September. Meantime, Dorissa was to go into training and Pat and Delila were to set up a series of engagements, small explosions that would lead up to the big bang in Atlantic City. Delila wanted Dorissa to share her luxurious penthouse, but Dorissa insisted on living in her own humble apartment, where she could commune in solitude with her plants and her Avocado Tree. She felt she needed plenty of energy to handle the demands of her growing career, and so she often visited Stanislaus' studio to be re-energized in his orgone pyramid.

It was a rigorous schedule: mornings with Stanislaus, who had appointed himself her technical adviser and psychic masseur; afternoons dancing with her Avocado Tree; evenings strategy planning with Pat and Delila, occasional meetings with Noah to gather his artistic advice, and letter exchanges with Juanita in prison to talk soul. Dorissa became so engrossed in her work that she lost all sexual desire. She became a sexless sensualist, enjoying Stanislaus' massages, eating sensual fruits and vegetables, smelling flowers and organic incense, feeling textures, gazing at colors and brindled skies, listening to the music of sound, and worshiping the

Great Goddess Earth, with her sensuous dance movements. She wasn't exactly sure she was in control of her life or sanity, but with her bevy of characters shoring her up, she reasoned she didn't need sanity. She allowed herself to be swept along on the enthusiasm of everyone else, taking the best ideas from each and incorporating them into her psyche. All the while she felt she was keeping close communion with the Great Goddess through psychic dance trances with her Avocado Tree.

Devoid of any obsessive sexual desires, she felt she became part of the Great Androgyne, a more omnipotent spirit that could understand more because it was neither of one sexual stereotype nor another. She could experience emotion as deep as a woman's birth canal and feel as cocksure as a male. She'd wrestled enough with her own gender to transcend it and develop a mercurial one. Dancing with her body, she'd emerged from it to empathize with all human bodies, regardless of their organs. Empathy, she decided, was the Great Mother of love and required an imagination unsquelched by social conditioning. Like Stanislaus Yeski's hero Wilhelm Reich, she believed that human genitals must cease to be the workhorses of nations. Freeing herself of sexual repression, she'd freed herself of any desperate need for sexual contact. More than ever before, she concentrated on her social conscience. Alive in her senses, she felt she might really have the power to make a difference in the world.

One day, as Stanislaus recharged her, they planned an electronic scheme to insure her success. He promised to engineer a sensorized sound tape. Its frequency vibrations would be designed to tickle the psychic plasma of her audience's navels and get them to join her in her belly-rolling ritual.

"As long as it's harmless and only inspires *dance*," she agreed.

When she confessed her affinity for the plant kingdom, he confessed he'd built a Plantolizer that could measure the emotional reactions of plants to animal stimuli. He promised to engineer an encased transistorized electrode that could be inserted into her to convey her orgastic dance ecstasy to her Avocado Tree. The Avocado, via its psychic plasma, would register its emotional reactions on the galvanometer of his Plantolizer.

Delila Dandi incorporated Dorissa and invested money in the

corporation. As executive director of Femfunelli, Inc., Delila was the belly dancer's personal manager. Bored with her jet-set dating service, she found the perfect diversion in Dorissa. Delila had always wanted to be the power behind a *woman's* throne. Turning her self-aware classic penis envy into a Svengali complex gave her a sense of phallic power. She was a high-class hustler, and she knew exactly what she was doing.

Pat Campley, as the executive booking agent for Femfunelli, Inc., became inseparable from Dorissa and Delila. It was his dream come true. Getting to "hang out" with the girls was all he'd ever wanted out of life. If he could make some bread while doing so, it was gravy on the roast beef, whipped cream on the pie, duck sauce on the eggroll!

Noah Levi-Museman advised Delila and Pat on artistic PR tactics. He was still not sure of Dorissa's sanity, but now that she'd danced successfully at Woodstock and become incorporated, he was convinced it didn't matter, especially since Pat Campley's office had begun to receive many invitations for her to appear as a spokeswoman of feminism, nonviolence, and ecological sanity.

Dorissa, feeling sure her sanity didn't matter, found her world flipping into place like a record label on an assembly line. Still she was tortured by the prospect of losing Chrysta to Oliver. Each time she visited her mother-in-law's to see the child, Dorissa returned home ever more fearful that she might lose her daughter forever to Oliver's repressive ways.

Dorissa convinced Delila to get her jet-set lawyers to bail Juanita Pietri out of prison. Temporarily freed from Rikers Island, Juanita appointed herself Dorissa's private soul guard.

"Don't worry, honey. You'll keep your baby with your heart! When she grow up, she know who her mama is!"

Juanita's earthy jargon had begun to permeate Dorissa's own speech, as did Noah's artistic aphorisms, Pat's fervent humor, Delila's witticisms, and Stanislaus' logic and scientific expostulation. Though daily growing more sophisticated, Dorissa was still as impressionable as ever. She became a conglomeration of all their mental acuities. Each day she became more and more capable of saying the right and entertaining thing into whatever microphone happened to be thrust before her open mouth. Perhaps, by the time Oliver's case came to trial, she'd be ready to argue persuasively before the judge.

One morning, as Stanislaus clamped the electrode of his Plantolizer onto Dorissa's Avocado Tree, she urged him eagerly,

"Let's get on with the experiment!" Then she lay down on his water bed and lifted her legs in the air. He inserted his smooth, lubricated, soft-plastic-encased, transistorized electrode into her inner sanctum.

"Oh, that feels good!" she sighed.

"I used a soft, skinlike plastic case," sighed Stanislaus, proud of his handiwork. "Now, as you dance, you will commune with your plants and it will register reactions on my Plantolizer."

"Oh Stan, this is one of the most exciting moments of my life," she sighed with ecstatic anticipation. "I'll be dancing to the Earth Mother, through my body to the Earth's energy source, the photosynthesizing, vegetal world! I'll be dancing in absolute communion with my darling Avocado Tree. Oh Stan, I'll be spiritualizing my body! Noah says that Carl Jung says the archetypal tree is symbolic of the highest spiritual attainment. Remember what Indian medicine man Bill Schenectady said? 'Pray to a tree every day to keep the Earth happy!'"

As Dorissa danced *au naturel* in Stanislaus' studio, he watched behind the glass window of his control booth and kept an eye on his galvanometer. Her energy impulses, skipping from synapse to synapse up and down her spine, quivered the needle on his machine. Perhaps the Avocado Tree was using the electrified moment to communicate its message from the Great Goddess Herself. The Tree, with a voice like Billie Burke, reassembled thoughts within Dorissa's brain as she danced entranced with it.

"Take my wisdom and use it to make peace among the symbiotic animal, vegetable, and spiritual kingdoms. Help keep atmospheric balance. Give the creative energy to save humanity from technological folly and false progress. Win enough media power to communicate with the masses. Channel the strength of women and help them tame the haphazard greeds and aggressions of men. Make a new garden of America, a luxuriant place of sheltering trees and glorious fruits, a place rich with Earthy comforts!"

119

implored the Tree of Dorissa's body and Dorissa's body of the Tree.

Stanislaus had several mental orgasms as he watched the needle of his Plantolizer register its erect and quivering excitement. As Dorissa danced with his transistorized electrode in her, he, in his glass booth, juggled the science of sound and psychic energy, serendipitously syzygyzing the discoveries of Thomas Edison, Carl Jung, Wilhelm Reich, Semyon Kirlian, Clive Backster, and others with his own peculiar genius.

"There is in all things an orgone of sound, brain, light, waves, ultrasonic and subsonic, subject to a universal law of physics," he concluded. "That universal law of physics is a cosmic orgasm, good feeling, love. I'll be the voice of sanity. I'll send my subliminal sound into all the receivers of America via her most powerful communications signal, the Pentagon's black box. I'll zap into Ma Bell, tap into the Pentagon's black box, and flip my switch at a frequency that bypasses the human ear and goes directly into the brain. No one will be the wiser."

Perhaps Stanislaus' alpha waves began to mix with the Avocado Tree's and Dorissa's, via the Earth Herself. They all sighed in unison as a nonverbal thought conglomerated in their psyches, "Love is the universal principle of physics!"

Having exhausted its communion with the vegetal world, Dorissa's body ceased dancing and sank down on Stanislaus' water bed. The bed rocked gently, making the needle on the Plantolizer swing in rhythm with her womb. Stanislaus, thrilled by the success of his experiment, grabbed her exhausted body in his arms. "It's a revolutionary moment in the history of human evolution!" he shouted, hugging her like a brother hugs a sister.

"Yes!" she agreed. "My whole body feels spiritualized!" Then she quickly dressed and hurried off for a meeting with Rosalie Steinbauer.

Rosalie had arranged for Dorissa to test her dance before her first real feminist audience, The Alliance Opposed to Rape, in the basement of a large Greenwich Village church. The performance would benefit a young woman who had been molested in the back of a Jewish delicatessen. The woman was fighting a civil suit against the proprietors of the delicatessen, who had refused to come to her aid in making a citizen's arrest. She'd been bending over the cream cheese and bagels just as the culprit decided to bump up against her posterior with his erect dill pickle and rub so hard that she fell into the dairy case, smashed the Philadelphia Brand cream cheese, and sprained her wrist. She had asked the store manager and his helpers to detain the man while she ran after a policeman who could make an arrest, but the store personnel had stood around stony-faced among the bialys looking at her as if she were hysterical, refusing to come to her aid.

She was so infuriated by the whole incident, especially since she'd been a good customer of the deli for years, that she filed a test case with the help of the American Civil Liberties Union. Newspapers reporting the case ignored the serious legal questions she raised. The newspapers were more interested in the fact that she was a very attractive woman in a miniskirt, implying that she got what she deserved. They made a mockery of the entire case.

As a result of the hostile coverage from newspaper reporters who made sport of her, she'd received hundreds of obscene calls and nasty visitors. Her nerves had been worn to a frazzle. She lost her job and her health, and she couldn't sleep at night. Now she needed money to continue financing her suit and to launch a campaign for legislative action against molesters and their abettors. The case had become known as Cynthia Strifle vs. Hiam Grumbaker's Delicatessen.

Dorissa was excited to think that she would appear that very Friday night before her first real feminist audience. She wondered why, with all the horrifying facts and statistical truths she'd read about in feminist paperbacks or seen reported on Educational Television, this rape case with a pickle rated benefit status over other more horrendous incidents, but she reminded herself that in the course of justice, trivial trial cases often end up in Supreme Court changes, making legislative history.

"It's probably that Cynthia Strifle is the only one around with enough balls to get something going. That's how Juanita would put it!" Dorissa concluded.

Most of the important radical feminists in the New York movement would be present at the benefit. She knew it would be "trial by fire," and she wished Stanislaus' sensorized sound tape was finished. She felt she could use a little help from technology, but Stan had run into a few snags. He promised, however, that he would have his tape ready in time for her big Atlantic City engagement. Meantime, she'd have to continue to depend on her own aura and sheer showmanship.

Delila accompanied her to the radical church and helped her change into her costume in an underground press office adjacent to the basement performance hall. As usual, Delila had seen to it that the media would be present. As she hooked Dorissa's belt into place, she backed the dancer belly to belly into the printing press and sighed deeply; then she gently inserted her middle finger very carefully up into Dorissa's inner sanctum.

"Oh dahling, you're simply beautiful. Remember that! You'll win them over with your charm and grace. I'll be right there in the front row sniffing my finger and getting all warm and runny watching you dance!" Delila remained ardently in pursuit of Dorissa, but the dancer was always too preoccupied with her work to comply. Somehow she didn't mind Delila's romantic fervor just before performance time. Delila made her feel so perfectly acceptable as a woman with a woman's body and aroma that her dancing thrived on the psychological support the charismatic woman offered.

Finally, Dorissa entered the church hall and delivered a rable-rousing speech, structured by Rosalie Steinbauer, peppered with homely wisdoms by Juanita, and laced with symbolic aphorisms by Noah. The New York feminists seemed to like what she said. They shouted and cheered every time she mentioned the word "woman" and booed and jeered every time she used the word "man." Then she doffed her robe and began ringing her finger cymbals with all the fervor she could muster. When she came to the part of her dance where she tossed her veil away, she noticed that several women in the audience whispered to each other.

"Look, she shaves her armpits," said a naturally frizzed and hairy-legged young woman in the front row.

"She can't be for real!" answered her companion, resting her hands on her head and displaying two hairy armpits.

Dorissa wasn't sure what was happening, but she noticed that the women began standing up, shouting, and debating with each other. Soon the hall was buzzing with subdued brawls and loud whispers as Dorissa, in her beaded bra and chiffon skirt with jingling belt, danced onward. After her dance, in which only half of the women present joined her, she was puzzled and offended. She went home totally distraught.

The next morning, Rosalie called to give her the verdict. The press coverage had ignored the meaning of the benefit for The Alliance Opposed to Rape. The reporter from the *Daily News* made the evening into an armpit issue. He quoted some of the women leaving the hall. The headline read: "Should Topless Battery Park Belly Dancer Shave Her Feminist Armpits?"

Dorissa was appalled. All her sincere efforts had been overlooked in favor of her armpits. The *Post* headline read: "Femfunelli Feminism a Hairy Issue." The *Daily News* heralded: "Feminist Belly Dancer Berated for Shaven Armpits." *Majority Voice* questioned: "To Shave or Not to Shave, That Is the Question!"

"You'd better not shave for the NOW Conference in Atlantic City, or the media will nail us to the cross by your armpits again," Rosalie insisted. "No matter how serious we try to get about it, the media men always drag the Movement back into the men's john and portray us arguing with the urinals. Every time I try to get some serious, sedate, and intellectual issue across or get some women's civil rights bill passed in the legislature, I can't get any publicity at all. You shave your armpits and belly dance and the whole MCP world comes running to snap your picture. But we'll use it to our best advantage yet! Maybe a religious cult of Goddess Earth is exactly what is needed to make this society healthy again. Still, you'd better let all your natural fuzz grow and chuck the harem costume. We need all the sister solidarity we can get! We've got to give you a real feminist image: work shirts, blue jeans, pant-suits!"

Dorissa felt disillusioned. She liked her feminine costume. It was as ancient as femininity itself. She figured the long-flowing skirt had probably been invented by some prehistoric woman to make the dance more graceful and lovely. "I really thought they'd understand what I said about the social devolution of women paralleling the downfall of her sacred rituals, but they got me by the armpits instead. They didn't get the whole idea of the Earth Mother's second coming! People sure get off on the damndest things!" she concluded, hanging up the phone with ex-prostitute Juanita's favorite saying.

As she discussed with Juanita her discouraging performance for The Alliance Opposed to Rape, Juanita's eyes lit up. "I think you oughta be the star attraction of the Black Puerto Rican Day Parade down Central Park West! I know just the folks in Spanish Harlem who would dig it!" She slapped her thigh and laughed heartily, attempting to bring Dorissa out of her blue funk. Juanita's enthusiasm was infectious.

"Maybe you've got something there!" Dorissa watered her Avocado Tree with organic fertilizer. "I'll call a meeting of Femfunelli, Inc., and we'll get to work on it right away!"

Annually, since the midsixties in Manhattan, floats and marching bands paraded along Central Park West celebrating Black Puerto Rican Day. Hot rice and beans, *tacos* and *soul foods* of various sorts were sold with rum and Pepsi-Cola along the edges of the park by family vendors in home-made pushcarts from Spanish Harlem. Juanita knew a well-to-do businessman in Spanish Harlem who owned a credit union. He helped to sponsor the parade every year. Juanita had grown up in the streets with him. He'd graduated from dope peddling to money lending. It was decided that Dorissa would dance in the parade on a float designed to celebrate Third World women. Stanislaus prepared a tape of Spanish-Afro rhythms.

If she were lucky enough to reach some black Puerto Rican feminists with her dance, the radical white feminists would be forced to take Dorissa more seriously into their ranks. If she could pull it off, she, herself, would be one of the very few Italian-American women to emerge from Mediterranean dogmas of male supremacy and join the ever-changing hierarchy of the disorganized women's liberation movement.

When parade day arrived, Dorissa, dressed in a bare-midrifted, red-satin Spanish flamenco costume, big black Afro wig with African hoop earrings and red platform shoes, stood rolling her belly on a huge flower-covered float, making its way slowly along Central Park West. The float glided past thick crowds of men, women, and children eating sizzling foods and gurgling beverages bought from family vendors who sold their folk recipes from home-made pushcarts. Across Dorissa's float in big red, black, and yellow letters were the words "The Birth Dance of Liberation for Third World Women."

Juanita and all her friends from Spanish Harlem were there to make the proceedings merrier. Dancing came naturally to them. They followed behind the float shouting and bumping their hips.

Take two moderately slow, gliding steps and bump your hip twice, pushing it out to the side quickly in double time. Take two more glides and double-bump your other hip. Continue with vigor, gliding and double-bumping for joy!

As cheering crowds joined Dorissa, dancing down the avenue with her, she communed with the trees of Central Park. She thought of how men had chipped New York City out of stone with the chisel of human greed. Cranes, piledrivers, steel cables like cocks shoved up and down elevator shafts had raped the Earth of Her vegetal wealth and left only a patch of green in the center of Manhattan Island. They'd feared visceral Mother Nature so much that they'd dressed uniformly in black frock coats or gray flannel suits like soldiers fighting a financial war against Her body.

"What this city needs more than anything is vegetation! More trees would improve the disposition of harried people, remind them how they come and go from Nature Herself!" said Dorissa into the microphones thrust before her as she shimmied and rolled her belly beside her Avocado Tree, which accompanied her on her float, parlaying her Earth worship to the trees of Central Park.

The black Puerto Rican men and women along the avenue were not the least bit disturbed by her armpit fuzz. Few of the women in the crowd had fallen prey to the Lady Schick industry, though transistor radios were rampant. When Stanislaus' sensorized sound tape failed its first trial run, the enthusiastic crowd co-operated by turning on and tuning in to the same ethnic radio station. Dorissa danced on to their transistorized music, joined by teeming, undulating throngs of people lining the avenue.

The publicity from the event featured her picture with parade crowds surrounding her, on the front of nearly every city newspaper. She smiled and waved from her flowery float. The speech she coauthored with Juanita and delivered into media microphones scored some important points for the social syndrome of women living on welfare in New York City. The radical white feminists were impressed. Rosalie called to congratulate her, saying she was more eagerly awaited at NOW's Atlantic City Conference than ever.

Day by day, Dorissa got hairier and shrewder. She had done the Black Puerto Rican Day Parade against the protests of Delila and Pat. They hadn't wanted her to waste her energies on the minority culture, but they had to admit that the media conveyed the correct message for a change.

Whether from her growing fame or Stanislaus' orgone accumulator, there was no doubt that Dorissa had become a pro at harvesting the energy with which to greet the task before her. She was ready for Atlantic City, and so was her Avocado Tree.

The night would soon arrive. Trial by water. Rosalie wasn't sure it would work, but she was willing to risk all for the sake of media coverage for her cause. Dorissa had been briefed to get in the three major political resolutions of the National Organization for Women: "equal pay for equal jobs; government day-care centers; peace and amnesty for all war protesters and for women in prison for illegal abortions."

Would she sink or swim along the shore of the North Atlantic, the giant ocean ruled by the Moon Goddess of Earth's menstrual cycle?

STEP 14:

The Gliding Walk

The convention hall was ablaze with lights and expectations. Dorissa stood in the curtained wings of the stage of the Chalfonte-Haddon Hotel, a notoriously elegant ocean resort of the twenties. Its windows overlooked the famed Steel Pier and Boardwalk of Atlantic City, where salt-water taffy had been invented a half century before. "Where the salt water brings out a lady's charms, in romantic, enchanting Atlantic City, down by the ole New Jersey shore."

Ms. Femfunelli, brazen feminist from New York City, had stopped shaving her armpits and legs, and let her hair go as wild as Janis Joplin's. She wore no make-up, not even a touch of mascara. She was scrubbed and washed in organic mustard-seed soap. Her hair was washed in Essence of Heather shampoo. A long, green, tie-dyed chiffon scarf was looped through her hip-hugger jeans to hold them up when she shimmied. She wore a minihalter, bought in a feminist boutique. It was appliquéd with female biological signs: the little circles with the crosses underneath.

Dorissa had, more or less, allowed Nature to take Her course. She'd grown several pounds thinner since the day she'd observed herself in the mirror of Aneera Ohanian's Studio of Middle Eastern Dance, but she'd accepted the fact that she would forever be a woman like those found on canvases of Rubens or Titian, not like those found in *Vogue*.

Also, in the wings, Stanislaus Yeski sat, finger poised, ready to switch on his newly perfected sensorized sound tape.

Dorissa peeked out through a crack in the stage curtain that separated her from her audience. The National Organization for Women awaited her, while a few yards down the Boardwalk, in another elegant hotel of the twenties, Miss America's television pageant was in full swing. Young woman after young woman was displaying her down-home, amateur talent. Dorissa spied Stella Babzug, feminist congresswoman. She sat in the front row, her jaw firmly set. Beyond her wide-brimmed hat was a sea of seething heads. Two thousand women filled the convention hall, and their "women's rights balloons of red, white, and blue rose like fat flower petals, above faces seeded with human eyes.

Alongside Stella Babzug sat Delila Dandi, dressed in a black suede pant-suit with ermine collar. She brandished her mother-of-pearl cigarette holder.

Pat Campley whispered and giggled into Delila's ear as he sat beside her in the front row. He was dressed in tight blue jeans and a Givenchy T-shirt, tinted aviator glasses, and a blond Afro wig from Bloomingdale's Hair Salon. He looked every inch the woman he wasn't. Juanita Pietri sat gazing straight ahead of her as Bill Schenectady, Indian medicine man, spoke into her ear, causing her to nod gravely in agreement with everything he said. Noah Levi-Museman sat beside him, impatiently leafing through a copy of *Opera News*, waiting for the show to begin. Stanislaus sat nimbly awaiting his cue to throw the switch on his newly perfected sensorized sound. Stella Babzug had just finished a brilliant speech denouncing some of the inequities wrought by male politicians. Her words had been met by volleyed cheers from different parts of the convention floor: "Amnesty for all women in prison for illegal abortion! Castrate the rapists! Peace on earth, good will to women!" Stella would be a hard number to follow.

Dorissa looked at the stage platform that had been erected in the convention hall. The Chalfonte-Haddon Hotel of Atlantic City was accustomed to hosting ladies' fashion shows and businessmen's conventions. A narrow walkway stretched out into the audience from the middle of the platform, the path along which Dorissa Femfunelli was to belly dance, just as the newly crowned Miss America walked the path of televised pageantry. Suddenly Dorissa heard the voice of Rosalie Steinbauer introducing her.

"Now the overnight sensation of the Movement in America, belly-dancing priestess of feminism, Dorissa Femfunelli!" boomed Rosalie's amplified voice throughout the convention hall. Dorissa gave Stanislaus the okay sign and he flipped his switch. Then she ran onstage to a synthesized drumroll of dumbeq quality. Its frequency vibrations were designed to wake up the audience by making their eyes blink rapidly. Two thousand women simultaneously blinked their eyes to open them wide upon Dorissa, who glided up to the microphone. She took the mike from its stand and held it close up to her lips. She spoke in a quiet, understated voice, with as sensual a tone as she could manage. She looked like a singer about to introduce a torch song, but instead she launched with subdued dignity into her speech.

"Men have always thought of women as the darkness, the ignorant passion, the irrational sex to be feared. They have been frightened by the moist caves of our bodies, even though they are anxious to come into them," she began. Behind all of her hours of rehearsing, sensorized sounding, aura building, thinking, hoping, planning, and working for this moment was her motherly desire to keep from losing her child, the fruit of her womb. She continued in a quiet, steady whisper, talking directly into the mike.

"They think of us as helpless wives, or young girls in bathing suits, dependent on prizes bestowed for breast and hip measurements. They have characterized Mother Nature as a scatterbrain, despised Her really, but put up with Her, as the child puts up with the mother though he yearns for freedom. We've been the receptacles for the thrusting bombs produced by their abstract in-

129

tellects. The patriarchs have made fools of women and debased the Earth Mother's body, clitorectomized and polluted it with their fear and greed. We must show them how to *feel* again. They are hustling after the kind of money they don't even need in order to enjoy the real pleasures of this Earth: a walk beside the clear sea, a glance at the setting sun, the smell of a field of flowers, the look of an autumn ablaze with the glory of Her vegetable kingdom. We must pray to Mother Nature again through the trees. She will have Her Second Coming as surely as we will learn to have ours. The patriarchal world is caught in the vice of fear. Mother Nature is not a lovable scatterbrain. She is Goddess. She sustains our bodies and gives us life. Men have forgotten the poems of milk that are our breasts and made them into cheap toys of mere lust."

Dorissa paused in the midst of her sensual whisper, and the mike amplified her huge and sincere sigh. Then, increasing her volume, she went on: "We are not toys nor hysterical scatter-brains! The feminine psyche in all of us, men and women, is the part of the human race that guards its *feelings*, and only with feeling can people learn compassion for one another; only through feeling, through the senses, are we alive. 'The Woman-Soul leads us on!'"

She paused again and a scattering of quiet applause went up here and there from the intently listening crowd. She was getting to the intellectuals with her poetic flights and keeping the more earthy intent with her sensual whisper.

She paused again, hushing the audience with anticipation. "I'm reaching the philosophic intellectuals via Noah and the women worshipers via Pat!" she thought. "Now for the cultural sophisticates via Delila and Juanita!"

Raising her voice a few more decibels and nearly swallowing the mike the way a rock singer might, Dorissa went on: "When I dance my New Dance of Liberation, remember, sisters, that it's a woman's dance, an ancient pagan rite in worship of Earth Herself, the Great Goddess of psychic feeling in the flesh! An early women's mystery! A magic birth dance of *wicca!* In its devolution to a sexist spectacle in the cafes of modern cities, it represents a cultural parallel for the devolution of the female from free and ac-

tive, lusty being to sex object! That's why we have got to turn it
all back around again for old Mama!"

Those less intellectual and culturally sophisticated members of
the audience who had begun to yawn, perked up in their chairs as
Dorissa came to a moderate crescendo on the words "sex object."
A cheer and universal round of applause went up from all.

"Now for Pat's pazzaz!" she thought.

"So at the end of my belly dance, I want everyone of you to get
up on your feet, roll your bellies, and join me in the aisles, because we're going to dance right out of here and down the boardwalk to the Miss America Pageant. We're going to show those
news cameras how real women strut their stuff. We will dance
like our ancient female ancestors, who were worshiped as divine
givers and nurturers of life. With the direct, erotic, honest gestures of our own folk art, we'll dance of a time when women were
not second-class drudges in a disposable, automatic, decadent civilization built upon ecological disaster and war machine finance.
We will dance of a time when we knelt on the Earth in full control of our muscles, pushing new life from our womb, not
strapped down on a male gynecologist's table, anesthetized, feet
in stirrups, so that *he* could pull the infant from our womb and
become, himself, the Great Deliverer! Dance the dance of the
Great Mother of us all! An orgastic birth dance!"

Wild applause and cheers went up from the crowd as Dorissa
reached the culturally, economically, and politically sophisticated,
including Stella Babzug, who sat smiling benignly under the wide
brim of her hat.

"Now for the final Juanita punch," thought Dorissa, taking a
tight grip on the mike. "I've got to bring the general rabble
around." She bellowed in a deep voice, like a red-hot Sophie
Tucker:

"Remember, the birth dance is ecstatic because the moment of
giving birth is, like death, an *orgasm*." She knew that that word
would wake up the nodders. "You can really get off on it! When
you hear me audibly groaning or sighing, when you feel my female ecstasy, I hope you will feel your own power. Get off on
being a woman! Remember, sisters, I'm no Raquel Welch either!
If I can dance, so can you. To hell with the Madison Avenue

image of woman!" Dorissa tossed her wild head of hair, waved her arms above her head, displaying her armpit fuzz, and shimmied her ample belly. "Very few of us look like French models anyway. Who needs Chanel No. 5 to invite Mr. Clean for an afternoon over the sponge mop? How many of us look like the centerfold of *Playboy*; or the cover of *Ladies' Home Journal?* Why should our bodies be used to advertise the latest gadgetry of ecological disaster? WOMEN POWER IS EARTH POWER AND MUCH TOO GOOD TO WASTE!" shouted Dorissa in the final triumph of her speech. Wild applause and cheers went up from the entire audience. From the front row, Delila gave the okay sign. Pat hopped out of his chair, cheering and yelling "Up with the clitoris!" Juanita slapped her knee and shouted: "Right on, baby!" Noah clapped sedately, but he was smiling broadly. Stanislaus flipped his switch, as usual. His sensorized sound filled the hall with an inordinate number of decibels and blew the minds of the women who'd sat for two hours listening to political speeches.

"That speech was for the judge!" thought Dorissa. She knew that one good dance was worth a thousand words.

She quickly donned the finger cymbals handy in the back pocket of her hip huggers, and was ready for the kill. Rosalie had arranged that she would dance exactly at the prime time moment when the new Miss America was announced. With Delila's jet-set pull, the convention had secured a boardwalk parade permit from the city. Balloons and banners had been prepared for the event, each tailored with a "women's rights" slogan, especially for the occasion.

Dorissa danced like a wild shaman, tossing her head this way and that, letting the sensorized sound rhythms run up and down her body. Her birth mime was savagely orgastic. She projected sheer animal magnetism. Her pelvic performance was infectious. The women in the audience felt their own bellies and groins tingle from the sensorized sound frequency, which urged them to join the ecstatic priestess of feminism in her pagan ritual. The younger ones rolled up their T-shirts or tied up their denim workshirts to expose their bellies and began dancing as best they could, clapping their hands in rhythm with her finger cymbals. Soon the entire convention hall was as alive with dancing bodies as Central Park West had been a week and a half earlier. Dorissa knew there was no stopping her now. Carried away by the sensorized sound rhythms, she danced out along the runway. She could hardly contain her ecstasy. Her aura bloomed from her like a gigantic white rose of truth. Even Stella Babzug was impressed enough to rise to her feet and wiggle her anterior. Rosalie Steinbauer gave Dorissa the woman-power fist salute, and Dorissa knew she was in. The place was alive with thrusting hips and undulating bellies.

Dorissa was as high as she could be on her dancing. Unconscious images passed through her mind and communicated themselves to her Avocado Tree, which she had begun to transport with her wherever she performed. The Indian medicine man, Bill Schenectady, had been given the job of guarding it in his lap at this performance.

"Dance!" said her body to her Avocado Tree. "Dance is the sacrament of the Earth Mother! I love the way it slows my mind down to listen to my body . . . the way it makes my eardrums touch the music like drumskins . . . the way I feel my legs move with the air. . . . Dance is the sacrament of the Earth Mother because it reduces hostility . . . creates sensitivity to the moment. Dance will break the back of the coffee and alcohol industries. Dance the juice of the improvisational muscles listening to the spaces between sounds! Dance the trance of the primitive!" She shimmied and rolled her belly wildly.

"Here I come! I'm making culture shock waves with the belly!" announced the Earth Mother Herself, through the bioplasmic signals the Avocado sent coursing through Dorissa's body as she danced.

"I see America belly dancing!" Dorissa Femfunelli echoed Isadora Duncan. But that was as far as her subconscious warblings went, because she fell in a trance off the edge of the runway, onto the laps of two large lesbian radicals. They helped her to her feet and proceeded to carry her on their shoulders, marching her toward the doors. All two thousand women followed after in undulating procession. Stanislaus rolled a big transistorized amplifier on wheels and brought up the rear of the parade. His

133

sensorized music filled the salt-water night air above and beyond the Boardwalk.

Take long gliding steps, slanting the torso back toward the Earth. Walk swinging low, admitting to the Earth's gravity.

Out along the Atlantic City Boardwalk marched two thousand belly-dancing feminists, carrying balloons and parade banners. One big banner read: "Reclaim our bellies for the Earth! She's a woman too!"

"Women's Breasts Are Ecological Wonders!" read another.

"Down with Phallic Weaponry! Up with Clitoral Love!" read the red, white, and blue balloons amid which Dorissa was transported aloft on the shoulders of her two good-natured carriers, as if she were the champion of the football squad just after the big game was won. "Earth Mothers and Daughters: Unite!" began the chant, shouted in unison with hundreds of thrusting hips and rolling bellies.

Dorissa felt such a sense of total achievement mixed with religious fervor that she was transported out of her body as it bounced atop the women's shoulders.

She floated with the ocean mist, giving two thousand feminists the frizzies as Mother Nature lapped at the billboard-littered shore. Majestic waves crashed against the wooden pillars of a giant Sea and Ski Suntan Lotion signboard. Sprawled across the sign was a photograph of a tan, bikini-clad woman, who smiled down over the noisy proceedings with a perfect Ultra-bright smile. A large lighted clock, centered exactly over her navel, announced the appointed hour as ten.

Inside the Hilton Hotel, Bert Parks, master of ceremonies for the Miss America Pageant, was dismayed. The shouts and music coming from the Boardwalk outside the windows were actually drowning out his annual song: "There she is, Miss America, there she is, your ideal!" As he sang his famed lyrics, the young woman, just crowned with her golden crown, cried, overcome with emotion, as she paraded along the walkway to her throne, her ermine cape trailing behind her. She wept not so much for joy as for the fact that the hairy belly dancer from New York City, with naked navel, had upstaged her All-American good looks and media coverage. The gaping eyes of major network video cameras had turned in a *Ms.* direction, along with the newspaper reporters, at the very moment that she was crowned *Miss* America.

"Oliver will never take Chrysta from me now," thought Dorissa as outside on the Boardwalk she sat aloft on two women's shoulders and waved triumphantly into the many cameras winding in her direction.

STEP 15:

The Egyptian Head-and-arm Pose

Delila and Pat, good promoters that they were, lined up a couple of engagements immediately after Dorissa's Atlantic City success. They wanted to be sure to keep her naked navel on the television screens of America. Dorissa felt caught like a cog in the huge wheel of their scheme to create a lucrative and prestigious super-star. Not knowing exactly what to do next and emotionally depleted by Oliver's declaration of war over Chrysta, she crept back into her private spirituality and went along for the ride, tell-ing herself she would soon be ready to take a firm stand against their joint megalomania.

Her first engagement required her to dance for a large group of housewives in Milwaukee's cultural complex, a huge concrete-and-glass structure called Mecca. She flew to Milwaukee to discover that Mecca housed what some of Milwaukee's businessmen hoped would be a great commercial come-on for women. Toasters, elec-

tric curlers, and various home gadgetry, as well as packaged supermarket features, were on display throughout the exposition hall.

Rosalie Steinbauer had been in touch with Milwaukee's top
feminist leaders about the show. Together they had coerced the
producers of the commercial exposition, called "The Wide
World of Women," into using feminist entertainment for the big
event. The Action Task Force co-ordinator for Milwaukee's
NOW had marched into the exposition's offices and delivered her
threat. If the producers didn't invite Dorissa Femfunelli, shaman
of feminism from New York, all the feminist news reporters in
Milwaukee would rise to the occasion and expose the exposition's
commercial usury of women, nipping the businessmen's publicity
campaign in the bud.

When Dorissa appeared before Milwaukee's housewives, she decided to wear her regular belly-dancing costume, and made the
mistake of exposing her radical armpits. She offended not only the
shaving products sponsor of the exposition, but also several of
Milwaukee's housewives, who found her pits too pubic for their
tastes. Again, the armpit issue was raised by the press. Again,
Dorissa experienced a fit of depression after her performance, just
as she had after the benefit for The Alliance Opposed to Rape,
when she'd been chided for her clean-shaven pits.

The only good part of her Milwaukee trip occurred when she
got loud cheers for telling the women they had the buying power
to stop plastic pollution. They could insist on buying only fresh
vegetables and nutritious foods for their families, instead of chips
and doodles and sugar cookies. Their cheers seemed to indicate
they were ready to give up soda pop and frozen pizza, but shaven
armpits, never! "Ah well," thought Dorissa, "I'll have to make it
fashionable either to shave or not to shave. But which? That is
the question."

A mother and daughter team from New England had delivered
a lecture on self-help clinics, teaching the women of Milwaukee's
exposition about the cervix and os. They had showed slides un-
covering the mysterious knowledge of woman's inner sanctum.
Dorissa had thought the cervix with its tiny opening, the os,
looked plum-like and lovely. She had been glad, at last, to know
what it looked like. The feminist mother and daughter team had

been first to join her in her dance ritual and coax others to join in. They felt great empathy for her theories of the belly dance as natural childbirth therapy and joined her with their own fervent desire to win women's bodies back from the male-dominated American medical industry. Watching the mother and daughter lecture team dancing together had made Dorissa think of Chrysta. She longed to dance, for carefree joy, with her daughter again.

As Dorissa jetted back to New York, she despondently read about "The armpit issue of feminism" in the Milwaukee press and wondered if American women would ever understand the spiritual significance of feminism. *Anima* must temper *animus*. The female spirit needed to be brought, once again, into a system of checks and balances with the male spirit. Feeling had as much to do with human salvation as thought. Dorissa knew it was her job to wake America to feminine psyche.

No sooner did she arrive home than Delila and Pat announced another engagement to keep the press hopping. They wanted her to develop a strong national reputation. Next, she was to dance in Florida for the senior citizens of Port St. Lucy, an event sponsored by the Miami Board of Trade.

In desperation, before boarding the plane to Florida, she shaved only one armpit and decided to wear blue jeans with the beaded bra of her belly-dancing costume. She did not discuss doing so with Delila, Pat, or Noah. They all stayed at home to hustle the media at its center and didn't know anything about it until too late. Dorissa appeared on the eleven-o'clock news strangely attired: half belly-dancing woman, half denim kid, half hairy, half shaven.

"Diddle diddle dumpling, my son John, went to bed with one shoe on!" exclaimed Delila to Pat and Noah as they gathered around the set. "Oliver just got some more fuel for his case of insanity."

"I'm beginning to wonder if the poor dear girl hasn't really flipped her lid. She's become so unstylish!" sighed Pat.

"Either that, or she's learned that total freedom of spirit and imagination is the only way she will survive as an artist," said

Noah, philosophically. "In which case, she may create her own style."

"Let's hope," they all concluded.

When Dorissa arrived in Miami Beach, she was immediately wined and dined by some members of the Board of Trade that were sponsoring the senior-citizen event. They announced that they wanted to improve public relations throughout the state by sponsoring recreational events for Florida's elderly citizenry.

Dorissa had never been to Miami Beach before in her life. She was aghast! If Milwaukee's Mecca had been an ecological disaster, with its exposition of kitchen gadgets and plastic supermarket mentality, Miami was the Mecca of capitalist decadence. Nowhere did she see the *beach* of Miami Beach. Blue fluorescent-lit pools, neon imitations of French provincialism, concrete copies of classic Greek statues, pink plastic flamingos, gold lamé tiles and lucite, assimilated wood frames filled with cardboard reproductions of master European paintings were everywhere. The glorious palm trees were lost amid neon lights. Billboards littered the shoreline. Each hotel attempted to outjazz the next with its imitation design. The diamond strip of Miami was more like a rhinestone bikini bought at a Neiman Marcus basement sale.

When Dorissa's evening of wining and dining ended, she collapsed in bed, crumpling her white cotton pant-suit and removing her aviator glasses. Her sacred Avocado Tree was safe in its large traveling terrarium beside her bed.

"It's not a dog-eat-dog wilderness we plants want for humans," it murmured subliminally through her dreams. "It's not a neon greed either. What we want, priestess, is a truly civilized garden, a place where woman and man live together with harmonious nature surrounding them, a peaceable symbiotic kingdom of plant and animal, spirit and body. Not a brutal wilderness, but a pleasant ecological garden of truth!" It smiled deep within its roots as she got up and watered it.

Dorissa was to dance in a huge center for senior citizens located in a suburb of Miami. It was a poured-concrete structure with orange plastic window casements that had once been a frozen orange juice factory. It was now the recreation center for vast numbers of old people who occupied a cinder-block housing development in its vicinity. The entire community was titled "Swamp Valley Home for the Ageless." Dorissa suspected that under the glitter of poured concrete and painted cinder block lurked the greedy rip-off machinery of real-estate speculation.

A wry and drunken woman who served as secretary to the directors of Miami's Board of Trade had whispered confidentially in her ear the night before: "Don't let these business hoodlums fool you, sweetheart, Swamp Valley's recreational center is built on the quicksand of gelder greed. The alligators crawl up out of the polluted muck each night to eat up the senior citizens who haven't already been carried off by giant mosquitoes!"

Dorissa thought how much the woman's candor reminded her of Juanita's. Dorissa wished that Juanita were there to get her through the performance. Stanislaus was always too busy playing around with the mixers, levers, and dials on his sound board to be of much emotional support. She wasn't quite sure whether to go ahead with her plan to dance in the half-Salome, half-Janis Joplin outfit she'd chosen to wear. She wondered if the senior citizens of Florida would dig her irony. She'd given up trying to determine what result her actions would get from the media. "It" was a many-headed monster with a mind of its own. Its naked navel was its television screen, and heaven only knew what it might expose there.

Dorissa watched the ageless people of Swamp Valley assembling. They hobbled on canes, wheeled in wheelchairs, or ambled like "outpatients" into a terminal, Social Security clinic. Like any good showwoman, she keenly sensed the challenge of the unusual audience. The eyes of its aging faces shone like stars in moonlight. The lone women and men or enduring couples who filed in and took their places in blue plastic-and-aluminum chairs had no doubt repopulated the country with many younger bodies, children, grandchildren, and great grandchildren.

She looked at the women's wrinkled faces and thought how one day she would be old, too. She wondered if she would still be belly dancing when she was seventy; if she would still be surviving years hence; if Chrysta, as a grown woman, would visit her old mom. If so, she hoped it wouldn't be in this Florida home for the "ageless." She had seen an item in a local newspaper about an eighty-year-old man who had barely escaped being eaten by an alligator. Alligators, disturbed by the ecological imbalances of real-estate speculation, had been rummaging for food around the disposal shed of the housing complex. The elderly community was in danger of being infiltrated by swamp alligators in large numbers. Senior citizens would be easy prey for the upset swamp creatures, capable of moving at a speed of forty miles per hour on land.

Dorissa had been struck by the bizarre news story, the horrifying irony in the land where Ponce de Leon had hoped to discover the fountain of youth. She felt that the Earth Mother's spirit was sorely needed in Swamp Valley.

When the entire hall was filled and the crowd settled down, Stanislaus flipped his switch. His sensorized sound brought the audience to attention. Dorissa began her lecture. She talked about being alive in the present without regrets for the past or obsessions about the future. She talked about how there are no money pockets in shrouds, not even American ones. She praised the Earth and women and the spirit of the *anima* in men, sighed of rebirth and spiritual salvation, murmured of joy, and declared that "youth is wasted on the young," a sentiment easily accepted by her audience.

"There's no disgrace or shame in growing old. To be old is to have lived. We must learn to cherish and value our experience instead of depreciating it, like last year's model of car!" said Dorissa into her transistorized neck mike. The stage was decorated in the center by her Avocado Tree. It was wearing its electrode communicator, just as she was wearing hers. Stanislaus always thrilled at the thought of his transistorized electrode inside of Dorissa as she danced. He'd built a Plantolizer into his sound board so that he could watch the erect and quivering excitement of his galvanometer as she ecstatically rolled her belly. Her denim-covered posterior and her naked anterior shimmied to his synthesized drumrolls as she finished her speech.

"We must create a more humane society that maximizes the potential of everybody, regardless of age or sex or race. Then we will have authentic maturity, authentic liberation!" she whispered into her mike as her amplified voice caressed the fourteen hundred eardrums of her gray and balding audience, tickling their navels with anticipation.

"Dance with me and celebrate the *anima*, the spirit that is life-giver and nurturer, the great grand old Earth Mother!" She built to a crescendo, then whipped her finger cymbals out of the back pockets of her hip huggers and began to glide about the stage. As she danced, she displayed one shaven armpit and one hairy one.

Soon the old people were clapping in time to the music. Then, as she performed her orgastic birth mime, grunting and groaning into her neck mike, sighing and moaning her amplified frenzy, the crowd observed in hushed reverance. The old women, with their mustaches, watched with the pain of recognition on their faces. They understood the birth agony. It was like the death agony to come. The old men, with their sagging breasts, whom age had androgynized as much as the women, understood, too.

Finally, as Dorissa danced down the platform steps into the audience for her joyous finale, more than half the senior citizens automatically joined her in the aisles, swaying to Stanislaus' sensorized rhythms on creaking but willing legs. The juice factory was alive with dance. Even the feebler, restricted by corsets, back braces, or brassieres, made some attempt at rolling their trussed-up bellies.

Dorissa ended by dancing a duet of bellies with a ninety-year-old man who opened his shirt and let his rotund Earth Mother belly jiggle for the *life* of him.

As Dorissa read the newspapers with their glowing reports of her success with the senior citizens of Florida, she became resigned to the fact that her career would probably seesaw forever with ups and downs. The television reporters seemed to understand every word of her lecture when she talked about an Earth garden as alternative to a wilderness or a city. As a matter of fact, some young local "hippie do-gooders," the very next morning, organized a project called "Health Gardens for the Aging." Dorissa's appearance helped to generate enough enthusiasm to involve the senior citizens in their own produce and work collective. Instead of sitting around bored, several hundred old men and women would discuss the merits of organic fertilizers and fresh natural foods. They would watch seeds they themselves had planted begin to sprout forth with fresh vegetables and fruits for their retirement tables.

Dorissa could not come down from the spiritual high she experienced as a result of her Florida performance. Though her audience had danced feebly, their bodies had expressed freedom from past regrets and future hopes. They had been alive that afternoon, with her, as they danced celebrating Earth's *anima*, more than any audience she'd known. They had suspended all intellectual disbelief and danced.

One eighty-nine-year-old woman in a wheelchair had rolled into Dorissa's dressing room afterward to explain that she had seen Isadora Duncan perform one of her last public dances at Carnegie Hall, in New York, over a half century before.

"She had a spirit just like yours. It glowed in her face! Lit up her body! She sat on the floor wrapped in black velvet from the waist down, moved only her arms and her bare upper body!" said the woman in cracking tones of rapture. "Some people in the audience tittered. They didn't understand, but I knew what she meant when she danced that way, with just her arms and shoulders. I remembered it all this afternoon, just because of you, my dear." Her pronouncement made Dorissa's day complete.

At last, Dorissa had forever buried the armpit tissue of feminism. Now she could get on with the important work of revelation. The old people invested her with courage. They hadn't noticed her one hairy armpit or her strange costume. The women in the audience, many of them with hairy upper lips or chins, and the old men, many of them with no hair on their heads, weren't the slightest bit concerned with fashion. They'd seen its absurdities come and go. Dorissa became more fervent in her faith and expounded upon it to Delila and Noah, who became more suspicious of her behavior. Delila was jealous that Dorissa's spiritualism took up all her attention, leaving little time for sensual enjoyment. Noah was disturbed that the more time Dorissa spent with her corporate advisers, Delila, Pat, Juanita, and Stanislaus, the less time she had for him. Also, her hairy, increasingly "savage" appearance did not appeal to his aesthetic taste. It served to convince him that she was indeed falling off the deep end.

Delila, floating on the cloud of her Svengali success, minimized the ingredients of Dorissa's talent. Delila thought of the dancer as a superstar of her own making. She gave a huge radical chic party with Dorissa as guest of honor, and planned with Pat an international tour for her superstar. Dorissa Femfúnelli was as notorious throughout America as Lord Byron or Paganini had been throughout Europe. Everyone wanted to meet her and see what she was really like.

Dorissa felt most kinship, after her Atlantic City success, with Stanislaus and Juanita. They didn't make any demands on her. If she felt like an energizing treatment or a philosophical discussion there were no strings attached to the sheer relaxation provided. People were calling Pat Campley's office every day to engage Ms. Femfunelli for a performance. She realized she must get a grip on herself. She would need to arrange things so she could accomplish Earth's ends.

Meditating daily with her Avocado Tree, using Stanislaus' Plantolizer and transistorized electrode, Dorissa was sure her gift of stardom had come directly from the Earth Mother Herself and must not be abused. The spiritual meaning of her sacred dance must be kept intact or, she believed, there would be dire consequences. One afternoon, not long after her Florida appearance, as Pat Campley's telephones were buzzing with requests for interviews and he and Delila were strategically mapping out tours and raking in advance sales for Femfunelli, Inc., Dorissa had an idea of her own. It came to her just after she finished dancing in a trance with her Tree.

"You know what I'm going to do next, Stan, now that I've been to the mountaintop and have nothing to lose?"

"Find another mountaintop?" asked Stanislaus as he compared his most recent galvanometer reactions with previous charts.

"In Atlantic City, I met a feminist who works for the National Parks Service of the U. S. Department of the Interior. I'm going to get her to sponsor a dance tour of all the park preserves across this country. That's how I'll really commune with Goddess Earth and receive Her inspiration for what I'm to do next."

Dorissa inserted Stanislaus' transistorized electrode in place. "I think I'll start with Yosemite and end up in Yellowstone. If I dance amid all the natural wonders, like the Grand Canyon and

Niagara Falls and the giant redwoods, I'm sure to experience the finest enlightenment possible. How about it? Are you with me? We'll bring Bill Schenectady and Juanita Pietri with us! I'll give them equal billing and get them in on the act! I've got to get away from Delila, Pat, and Noah for a while. They're holding me back. Delila wants me to be a big, commercial, jet-set superstar! Noah wants me to calm down to his sense of aesthetics and become an *artiste!* Pat wants me to crash Hollywood and outshine the Sunset Strip. He spends all his spare time shopping at Bergdorf Goodman instead of worshiping at the shrine of the vulva. What I want is to be a celebrant for the Earth Mother. They just don't understand. Unless I can convince the judge of my moral fiber, I still might lose Chrysta to Oliver. What do you think? Anybody who's contracted with the U. S. Government is sure to look a little saner in the eyes of the judiciary!" She laughed and tickled Stanislaus.

Stand erect, feet slightly apart, raise arms high over head, palms together. Without bending neck, move head laterally, side to side. Be as much of a sphinx as possible.

"I'm with you, priestess! I've been with you since the day I first massaged your neck on that bus from Woodstock. You blew my mind with your philodendron body, and your vibes are the best I've ever come across. I think I understand where your head is at. Wherever you want to go is okay with me. As a matter of fact, I've got some of my own ideas for revolutionizing things."

"What is this secret project you've been working on, Stan? Why won't you tell me about it?" asked Dorissa, her curiosity piqued by his mysterious smile.

"You'll find out soon enough, priestess! It's a surprise!" answered Stanislaus, enraptured with the thrill of his own mischief.

STEP 16:

The Buttock Bump

Dorissa, as she'd hoped, acquired sponsorship from the Department of the Interior to tour the country's natural preserves and promote ecology. She also secured a letter from the chief government executive of the department requesting postponement of her court trial for custody of Chrysta until the completion of the tour. Her plan to bring her soulmate Juanita along failed, however. Juanita, with the help of Delila's jet-set lawyers, had come quickly to trial. A liberal judge, who took all her aggravated motives into account, sentenced her to only two years for highly motivated manslaughter. Bill Schenectady, Indian medicine man, was sorry to have to refuse Dorissa's invitation, also. He'd promised never to leave the reservation again, but he wished her luck and said he would be praying to the Earth along with her, wherever she went, across the land.

Meanwhile, Pat Campley was the happiest member of Dorissa's entourage. He was now able to crossdress publicly and wear his feminine clothes to the office every day. His office had been redecorated with pink vulva wallpaper designed by Narcissa Tittle, whose graphics were the hottest items in Soho. Chin Lo Slung's giant blowups of the body-painted Dorissa, with ferns and vines winding around her navel, adorned the wall of Pat's waiting room. Now that Mr. Campley was so successful, no one cared how he dressed or what sex he was.

Already, Femfunelli, Inc., was reaching over a million in assets. Dorissa spent a good deal of time running around to television and radio talk shows doing guest spots. She'd had to devise many wigged disguises, which Pat was only too happy to invent, to make her way around the city unnoticed by her growing numbers of fans.

A big record company wanted Dorissa to cut an album of grunts, groans, and orgastic sighs to Middle Eastern music for a phenomenal sum. Much to Delila's dismay, Dorissa had refused the offer. She planned to start her own record company, Earth Mother Recordings, Inc., to promote conservational ecology, and to make Stanislaus its chief executive. Delila, angry and jealous over Stanislaus' time and influence with Dorissa, devised all sorts of schemes for investing capital and firing Stanislaus as technical adviser to Femfunelli, Inc. Dorissa, shored up by Juanita, had stuck to her guns and refused to invest or to fire Stanislaus.

"I'll know where and when to invest when I return from my tour of the wilderness," she insisted, patting Delila tenderly on the cheek to mollify her.

Delila complained, "Really, dahling, if you insist on your spiritual purity, this little empire we're building is sure to collapse around our ears! You've got me worried with all this Earth Worship mania and that freaky sound engineer's peculiar experiments. There's no way to prove that you are actually communing with any Earth goddesses. Wake up to the real world, dear! Progress depends on capitalist greed, and only money really talks out there. If we don't invest in something sounder than an American bank soon, we'll be at the mercy of this crazy economy! Dahling, give me a nice long kiss for a change. I haven't made love with you in so long! You're driving me crazy! You're always off dancing with that damned Avocado Tree and Stanislaus' electrodes!"

147

Dorissa left Delila's penthouse feeling indignant. "How dare she damn my Avocado Tree! It's what put the vegetal kingdom behind this corporation! We have the Earth Mother to thank for my stardom, not her Battery Park scheme. I'm sure of that even if she isn't," thought Dorissa as she rode down the elevator.

Delila reluctantly consented to the National Parks tour, but insisted on throwing yet another chic party, a big bash to celebrate and launch the tour. All the top jet-setters and VIPs of New York, London, Paris, and Rome had been invited. Delila was in the process of maneuvering a command performance for her media star before the Queen of England. She hoped that all the rest of European aristocracy would thereby request to be entertained by her Trilby, too.

When the big party night arrived, Delila, smashingly attired in a red-and-black Yves St. Laurent gown, brandishing a long ivory cigarette holder, was in her glory, sipping French champagne and greeting her famous guests. Dorissa, to appease her charismatic manager, arrived in a dress designed especially for the occasion: a long, bare-midriff gown of sheer green chiffon with seashells and freeze-dried seaweed sewn into the bodice. She wore a leafy avocado branch, woven into a tiara around the crown of her naturally frizzed hair. Her armpits, the right shaved and the left unshaved, were prominently displayed. They were fast becoming her trademark. Young girls throughout the country had begun to imitate the Femfunelli style of one-side shaving. And necklines that plunged all the way down past the navel were the latest aphrodisiac of fashion.

Dorissa moved quickly through the crowd. She didn't want to be interrogated with the same dull questions by cocktail sippers. She herself never drank more than a glass of wine at dinner. To her, drinking hard alcohol was a decadent product of a guilt-ridden society, requiring huge polluting factories for its distillation. Death by drunken driving, she'd come to realize, was a bigger blight than cancer or heart disease. She preferred the peasant grass weed, marijuana, to any other drug, including caffeine. But dancing gave her the greatest emotional high.

As she drifted around the room, gracefully disengaging herself from this and that conversation, she realized that the search for

148

orgastic potency was really *in* among the well-to-do. More than half the conversations were sophisticated discussions of the finer psychology of sexuality. Everyone was in search of bigger, better, longer, and more frequent orgasms. "Orgasm" might very well be the next word that Robert Indiana would stylize for an American postage stamp or Peter Max put in day-glo letters on the front of T-shirts. The search for the "Big O" was really *in!*

Dorissa was amazed, looking back over her own life. Times had really changed since she was a girl! She realized that she'd not even known that women had orgasms until she was twenty-four and a mother. She floated through the sea of guests, pretending she was on her way to talk to someone in particular so as to avoid talking to anyone at all. She didn't want to explain for the fifty-fifth time why she dared to belly dance in the name of feminism. Older people always smiled benignly at her answer; younger ones tuned in and got off on the idea; gay men looked at her as if she were Bette Davis gone mad with women's lib; and attractive women looked at her as if to say, "My dear, I know very well why you belly dance. You want to attract all the attention away from the rest of us!" Men, of course, treated her very much like a sexy dancing star. They figured she was merely capitalizing on her belly. Lesbians courted her like a fem. Young men came on like Gang Busters. Other artists looked down their noses as if she were a commercial sellout. Commercial sellouts thought she hadn't sold out enough. Of course, there were those few who understood, but her fame didn't seem to depend on people understanding her, a fact that dismayed her. To combat it all, she simply replied with a soft answer that turneth away wrath, and explained that she was a sophisticated pagan, involved with sublime earthiness and not smut. Still, few got her message, it seemed.

Soon Dorissa found herself in need of solitude to quiet her spirit. A hot conversation with culture hero Seth Raider about his campaign against consumer frauds thoroughly exhausted her.

"How adorable he is!" she thought. "I'd love to get all involved with him for the sake of Mother Earth, but he's so serious about his work he didn't even notice I was flirting. Come to think of it, I'm so serious about mine, I'm not a very good flirt!"

She looked around and noticed her favorite counterculture

hero, famous, "beat generation" poet Zaddock Zinsburg. He stood locked into a corner by a small crowd of enthusiasts. He looked cornered and unhappy to be. She could tell by reading his body: His posture was defensive. His shoulders, raised like a cat's, were backed against the wall. She empathized with him. "He probably doesn't like radical chic parties either," she mused as she elbowed her way into the clique that surrounded him. He looked up and smiled beatifically, his dark eyes twinkling through his thick glasses, his spiritual smile poised above his long, black beard.

"Come out to the terrace and dance with me!" she whispered. "It's better than standing around chatting. I'll teach you how to belly dance for Earth!"

Before he knew it, Zinsburg was out on the terrace amid the shrubs, dancing with Dorissa. They slowly worked themselves into a Sufi trance, a contemplative high in which the fewest words communicated a world of meaning.

"Arise like a lamb!" he laughed, dancing.

"Forget the *Tibetan Book of the Dead!* Choose life; not fatalism!" laughed Dorissa, bumping her buttock against his as she mixed her literary references up with her shimmies.

"Turn the other cheek!" he retorted, giggling and thrusting his buttock at hers.

Take three steps, then thrust one buttock outward. Take three steps to the other side and bump the other. If a partner is available, you might enjoy bumping cheek to cheek.

Zinsburg and Dorissa intertwined spirits like gossamer threads. To dance with him was one of her fantasies come true. Soon he was jokingly teaching her the Yab-yum position of Tantric yoga. As they sat in Full Lotus gazing into each other's eyes, he laughed, "Shall we get married and invite the press?"

Dorissa laughed heartily at the poet's joke. "Gay beat poet copulates with bisexual priestess of feminism!" she rejoined. "The headlines would be great!"

"We'll use Walt Whitman's *I Sing the Body Electric* as our wedding prayer," he concluded.

At 1:00 A.M., the party still in full swing, Dorissa kissed Zinsburg, and they exchanged farewells. Both wanted to find a quiet place to meditate. They'd stimulated each other to new realizations. Dorissa drifted away from the crowd. Sneaking into Delila's bedroom, she closed the door behind her. She wanted to commune there with her Avocado Tree, a cutting from which Stanislaus had outfitted with a traveling terrarium complete with back pack and battery-driven grow lamp. It went with her wherever she traveled, a fact that dismayed Delila, Pat, and Noah. They suspected she'd really flipped out.

She knelt in solitude beside the terrarium and opened the lid to stroke the tree's leaves. She began to transcend the heady atmosphere of the party, reeking with French perfumes and political socializing. As she meditated in a transcendent state, Stanislaus quietly opened the door behind her and entered the room. He watched her in silence for a minute, then crept across the carpet toward her. Suddenly she was aware of his presence and turned.

"Stan, you startled me!"

"I just came to warn you. Some corporate shit is about to hit the fan! I wish Juanita were here now!"

"What do you mean?"

"Delila, Noah, and Pat are on their way in here. They have a pronouncement to make. They're looking for you. I hope you have the sense to resist. But I don't know. I saw you doing tantric hanky-panky with that poet out on the terrace! Maybe you're having fun and falling for all this superstar bullshit!" He felt jealousy but did not want to admit it to himself. "God, this party bores me!"

"Why are you so angry, Stan? I don't know what you're talking about, but I can feel your bad vibes!"

"I've been busting my ass working for you these past months, building your aura in my orgone pyramid, zapping you into your energy source, tuning you into your Avocado Tree with my Plantolizer. I hope you aren't falling for this superstar, radical chic bullshit! That's all!"

Dorissa felt magnetized by Stanislaus' body as he stood, his hands firmly on her shoulders. She looked into his eyes and he touched her cheek softly, then turned away, as if stopping himself. Before he could explain further, Delila, followed by stylishly clad

Pat and gentlemanly Noah, entered the room. Seeing Stanislaus alone with Dorissa immediately galled Delila.

"Stan, please wait outside! We want to talk to the priestess alone!" commanded Delila, imperiously.

Stanislaus knew better than to tangle with Delila Dandi. She was in charge of Femfunelli, Inc., and he had his own reasons for wanting to work under its logo. As much as he wanted to talk with Dorissa, he knew that he wasn't quite as indispensable to her as Delila, with her bevy of jet-set lawyers. After raising his eyebrows discreetly at Dorissa, he smirked as if to say, "I told you this was coming," and silently left the room.

Once the door closed behind him, Delila went to Dorissa and put her hands on the dancer's shoulders. "Look, dahling, we want to talk to you! We don't think you are doing the right thing. This tour of the National Parks is nothing compared to what you could be doing in Europe. If this corporation is going to be secure, it has got to reach across the Atlantic. I have some wonderful news! We just got a call this afternoon from Queen Elizabeth's chancellor of entertainment at Buckingham Palace. She wants you to come and perform for her. It's a world's worth of international media coverage!"

Pat chimed in excitedly. "Before you know it, priestess honey, you'll be performing for all the crowned heads of Europe!"

"Oh Pat, you're just saying that because Delila told you to. Now that you get to chum around with all the feminists and shop every afternoon at Bergdorf Goodman's, you couldn't care less what I do!"

Pat defended himself. "Oh come on, honey. Delila's right. The European tour is more important for the security of Femfunelli, Inc., right now, than a tour of the American wilds. You're already a smash here! You can do the parks some other year!"

"And you, Noah, what's your opinion?" asked Dorissa, already sensing that he would comply with Delila and Pat.

"Well, you could do much to broaden your acceptance as a serious dancer if you play some of the great concert halls of Europe, now. An appearance before the Queen of England is certainly more important for your artistic reputation than going around the wilds, dancing like a savage."

Dorissa knelt by her Avocado and stroked its leaves. She wished that Juanita were there to help her. After a long pause in which they all waited with baited breath, she spoke softly: "I know the European tour is important to all of you, but I can't travel around to the royalty of Europe until I've communed with my native land first. I can do more good here, right now. Americans are beginning to take my Earth worship seriously. In Europe, I'd only be considered a flashy American entertainment, like some rock star!"

"But sweetie-pie," said Delila, giving her a hug, "Europe will make your fame as immortal as Isadora's." She turned to Noah for support. "Isn't that so, Noah?"

"Of course. Isadora toured the concert halls of Europe," argued Noah.

"You've made your mark here, priestess honey!" whined Pat. "You're hotter than a frying pan. You can do Marv Gavett every night if you want. Everybody's wearing plunging bellylines. They are the latest thing!"

"We've got to strike while the iron is hot for world fame!" said Delila with great enthusiasm.

"No chinese fortune cookie told you that, Delila! I see dollar signs and social climbing in your eyes! You are very dear to me, and you've been very helpful, but I must do this parks tour, now. Working for the U. S. Government is the best way to appear legitimate before a U.S. judge. A judge who knows that I've been checked out by the CIA, or the FBI, as everybody probably is before signing a contract with the government, will surely decide in my favor against Oliver's plea for Chrysta!"

Delila sighed. "The Queen of England can certainly legitimize you, dahling! Don't be absurd!"

Pat agreed: "She sure is classy, even if she is a frump!"

Noah complied: "The concert halls of Europe are the thing for you now!"

"If I get a really radical judge, he's not going to be impressed by chic! I'm going to do the park preserves first, right here at home on my own turf! I don't say 'no' to the cities of Europe, but I feel I must do the American wilds *first*. I need Earth's wisdom."

She finished her little speech and knelt to stroke her Avocado Tree.

Delila lost her cool. "That damn plant. I think you love it better than any of us. Oliver's right. You have flipped out!" She kicked the terrarium hard enough to make its grow lamp black out. "You don't even know what's good for you anymore! I've already told the Queen you would come. I'm going to look like a fool!"

Dorissa was struck with indignation. She glared in disbelief at Delila. Pat stepped between them. "Now girls, let's not have any hair-pulling! Come on, priestess honey. Listen to us. We know what's best." As Dorissa looked him straight in the eyes, he lowered his. He knew that she was aware of Delila's coaching him, but he wanted to keep his place, cozy and warm, with Femfunelli, Inc. He reasoned that Delila had more business sense in her little pinky than Dorissa had in her whole belly.

Dorissa, clutching her wounded terrarium to her breast, looked at Noah. He shrugged his shoulders in despair. "You are getting a bit carried away with your Earth worship, my dear. I've been worried you were going off the deep end with Stanislaus and his electrodes. A European tour would be healthy for you right now. Delila and I will come with you." Noah's ambitions for Dorissa were usually in conflict with Delila's and Pat's business acumen, so he was glad to be in agreement with them for a change. If he could no longer have a sure place in Dorissa's bed, he wanted, nobly, to have a hand in steering her corporation toward the arts and culture.

Dorissa, in silence, looked around at all of them. They were staring at her as if she were a patient in a mental ward. They each tried to touch her affectionately, but she moved away from them. She felt cornered. They were telling her what to do, and it was in direct opposition to the signals she was getting from the Earth Mother. She'd always relied on their advice and, indeed, felt she would not have come as far as she was without them. She longed for Juanita's help now. The thought of Juanita comforted her anguish.

She clutched her Avocado Tree's terrarium and spoke softly and firmly. "I'm going on the parks tour. I'm sorry. I know you all mean well. I appreciate all the ways in which you've helped me, but I must do what I believe is right!"

"You can't!" shrieked Delila. "I've committed you to the Queen. We, your Board of Directors, outvote you!"

"Then have me arrested for going against Femfunelli, Inc., but I'm touring the American wilderness first!"

Stanislaus re-entered the room at an opportune moment. As soon as Dorissa saw him, she did exactly what he'd hoped she'd do.

"Stan, take me home. I'm leaving for Yosemite tomorrow morning, as scheduled. It will be good to get away from New York, where my friends have so much faith in my infirmity!"

Stanislaus grinned, broadly. He had his own black-box scheme for wanting to tour the U.S.A. "I think the parks tour is a great idea, priestess!"

Delila glared daggers at him. She was beside herself. She could only be happy as the entrepreneur of an international jet-set superstar.

"Wait, priestess," begged Pat. "Don't get all upset! You know we love you. You know how hard we've been working for you!"

Dorissa, without turning around, exited in a flutter of green chiffon. "Good night, Pat. Let me know if you make the gossip column shopping for blue jeans at Bloomingdale's with Rosalie!" Dorissa quipped.

Stanislaus, his gray-brown curls bobbing, followed after her.

STEP 17:

The Birth Dance of Earth

Before departing on her national tour, Dorissa visited Rikers Island to see Juanita, who would soon be shipped to a penitentiary. The Women's House of Detention brought back memories of difficult times. The communal Pelvic Thrust she'd taught Juanita and the inmates was still practiced as a subtle protest. The prisoners had not forgotten the feminist belly dancer's incarceration after her Battery Park arrest.

Dorissa spoke to Juanita in the visitors' center. "I'm not giving in to Oliver, Noah, Delila, or Pat," she promised her confidante.

"That's right, honey! I wish I could make the tour with you, but don't you worry none about me! I'm going to get through these next couple of years okay. I'll be out on parole before you know it!"

"When you're free, there'll always be a job with Femfunelli, Inc., waiting for you. You know that."

"Don't worry, Mama! You gonna get yo' baby back! That Oliver don't stand a chance after this tour!"

"I'm afraid he does, Juanita. Noah says I'm like Demeter in search of Persephone. It all depends on what godlike judge handles the case!"

"Well, honey, I'll be prayin' to the Big Mama upstairs for you!"

"You know, I'm seriously thinking of founding an Earth Mother society, a sort of antireligious spirituality that legitimizes the human body as its church of worship along with the Earth as the body's sustainer!"

"Well, I can dig that. A church you take everywhere with you, even to bed! You got yo'self a sale, honey!" Juanita's face managed a smile as she waved to the departing Dorissa from behind the thick plate glass of the electronically sealed visitors' entrance.

Before departing with Stanislaus for the airport, Dorissa breakfasted with Chrysta at her grandmother's. Partly to amuse her mother-in-law and partly because she wanted to inspire her child with reverence for the good things of Earth, she'd taught her a special prayer of grace. At every meal they shared together, they rolled their bellies and said:

Bless us, O Mother, for these our gifts that we are about to receive into our bodies from Earth, our bounty, ah women!

Dorissa told Chrysta that it was as much a prayer of thanks to Grandma for serving a good breakfast as to Goddess Earth for food to serve. Chrysta looked into her mother's eyes. She didn't exactly understand the explanations Dorissa offered for ordinary things, but she got a general feeling from them. Composed of enthusiasm, the feeling was not one of indifference. The child felt the world was good to be alive in, a place where everything derived its balance and meaning.

"I'm off to California to dance for some very old giant trees. I'll tell you all about them when I get back!" said Dorissa, affectionately bidding her daughter good-bye.

On the way to Kennedy Airport, Dorissa wept as she sat beside Stanislaus in his sound truck loaded with luggage and equipment

157

for the tour. With Juanita in prison, he was the only person Dorissa could confide in. Attracted by the bright star of her notoriety, several Johnny-come-latelys flocked around her, but she kept them at bay. Noah's fatherly protection and Delila's motherly warmth had insulated her from the world. Noah and Delila discussed her welfare as if she were their child. She felt a degree of panic now that she was setting out devoid of their emotional support.

"Oh Stan, maybe I'm wrong! Maybe Delila and Noah are right to think I'm flipping out. If I lose Chrysta, nothing will have been worth it!"

Stanislaus raised his brows and tossed his curls, "Listen, when we finish this tour, your reputation will be solid, baby! We are now working for the U. S. Department of the Interior. What judge is not going to be impressed by that? Once you get yourself a contract with the U. S. Government, you can be any kind of a nut and pretty much get away with it!" He grinned and patted her limp hand, reveling at the many telephone circuits he would come in contact with as they toured across the nation. Each would give him another zap into the black-box signal, and soon his experiment would be realized. "When we get back from this tour, we'll hobnob in Washington and see if we can't pull a few strings. You can bring it all the way to the Supreme Court if you have to, so don't worry!"

"But I want the whole thing settled quietly for Chrysta's sake." Dorissa blew her nose and looked out the windshield at the gray concrete highway, ornamented with green aluminum signs, stretching out before her. "Not a newsman in this country is onto the story, but if things get hotter, it could turn into a public mess!"

Dorissa danced her ritual across the country: from Niagara Falls to Yellowstone National Park, from the Great Salt Lake to the Grand Canyon, from the Painted Desert to Yosemite, finally arriving on the Pacific Coast of California in late November. She and Stanislaus had followed the tour the National Parks Service had mapped out for them. Each ritual staged in a natural setting attracted more news coverage than the last. Her growing notoriety was partly due to a rain dance she'd performed in the Midwest. It ended with thunderclaps and a downpour over parched farmlands suffering drought. Some of the farmers of Iowa were ready to swear she'd saved their corn crops with her ritual belly rolls. Many American naturalists were beginning to believe she possessed psychic influence with Mother Nature.

In Redwood City, an agricultural exposition was in full swing. Dorissa's appearance was scheduled to promote both the exposition and the giant redwood wonders of the county, and to celebrate Thanksgiving Day. The surrounding farmlands had been suffering from early frosts. Many farmers feared loss of their avocado crops before they could be harvested. Since the sun hadn't shined on sunny California for seven days, they hoped Dorissa's feminist Earth worship would save their harvests. Her rituals, reported upon almost daily by major newscasters, were the hottest news items.

In the midst of the redwood forests, beneath its tallest trees, a huge cornucopia had been constructed of straw and filled to overflowing with fresh fruits and vegetables. Dorissa was to dance out of the cornucopia onto a wooden platform erected in front of it. Several remote control TV cameras were scheduled to take in the proceedings and broadcast them live on major network news specials. The traditional Thanksgiving Day football games were to be pre-empted by her sacred dance among the redwoods.

"How absolutely lovely!" exclaimed Dorissa as the chairman of the agricultural exposition and the public-relations director of California's redwood preserves welcomed her, introducing her to the natural setting for her Thanksgiving Day dance. "I feel uplifted just thinking about dancing here!"

After a rigorous day of talk shows, Dorissa sat alone in front of the TV of her motel room. She felt her spirit in need of a lift. She was exhausted from ardent speechmaking, dancing, and travel. Though Stanislaus kept her in condition with acupressure, Shiatsu, and Reichian massage and helped her commune electronically with her Avocado Tree, she felt lonely. She missed Chrysta and Juanita, even Noah, Delila, and Pat. Though Dorissa often communicated with Chrysta and Juanita, she'd refused all messages, calls, and letters from Noah, Delila, and Pat. Dorissa didn't want contact with them, for they had shaken her faith in her own sanity and motivation. She wasn't sure exactly how to proceed without them, and she expected that there would be a showdown when she returned to New York. Delila would want to know exactly where and when she could invest the assets of Femfunelli, Inc., or else.

As Dorissa's power with the media grew, she became increasingly unsure of how to use it. She had always depended on Pat, Delila, and Noah to keep her informed of all feedback. With only Stanislaus for company on tour, she felt isolated. He was reticent and involved with his mysterious experiments, charts, sound boards, circuits, and transistors. Dorissa spent so much time in psychic dance communion with the Great Goddess that she longed for intimacy with another human. The Goddess Herself seemed to warn that too much solitude was counterproductive.

Unable to sleep, she went next door to Stanislaus' room and found him, as usual, fidgeting with his gadgets.

"What can I do for you, priestess?" he asked, hardly looking up from his work. He spoke in the same impersonal tone he always used when giving her a pyramid orgone treatment or a massage.

"I can't sleep!" she complained, standing over him.

"Want a massage?" he offered.

"No thanks. I just need someone to talk to."

"Too much work and no play?" he asked, looking up briefly to smile at her. Though he was not above using Femfunelli, Inc., as a cover-up for his own devices, he stopped short of insinuating himself into Dorissa's emotional life. He assumed that she was bisexually involved with Noah and Delila and committed to them. As he looked up at her she seemed, for the first time, lonely and dejected. "Want to make love?" he asked in a flippant tone, expecting that she was too preoccupied with her work and her mission to entertain the suggestion.

She decided he was merely being ironic. In the few months she'd known him, he'd never made a direct sexual advance. The only thing he had inserted into her was a transistorized electrode. She'd assumed he was some kind of genius loner, too full of science and disillusioned with imperfectable humanity to need intimacy with a woman. He'd told her that he'd been married to a rock star whose career he'd fostered. His wife had left him for a wealthier man. Dorissa decided that Stanislaus' protective cynicism was impenetrable.

"I get all the orgastic release I need from dancing! Pure sublimation!" She laughed nervously.

He fondled the gadget he held, plugging a wire into its socket. He didn't speak. Rejection was too painful to risk.

"What are you working on?" she asked.

"I'd explain, but I don't think you'd understand." He hooked his device to the telephone jack and placed a headset over his ears. Dorissa felt shut out by his earphones and gave up trying to talk to him.

She returned to her room, where she tossed and turned in her bed, fitfully unable to sleep, until she no longer knew if she was awake and dreaming, or asleep and living. She danced along a forest path into the woods of her own spirit. There, she imagined herself on a big turkey platter atop her father's dining-room table. Angelo Femfunelli was preparing to serve her as his Thanksgiving feast. Uncle Jimmy Honeywell threw dollar bills on the tablecloth as she roasted over a slow fire. Chrysta sat at the other end of the long table with her grandmother, saying grace to the Earth Mother over a plastic cup of yogurt. . . . Delila, beside her, sipped Chartreuse liqueur. She had brought a present for Chrysta . . . a plastic doll, a replica of Isadora Duncan, that walked, talked, ate, and defecated into a disposable diaper. . . . Dorissa told Delila that she shouldn't buy such ecological disasters, as the doll shit a nontoxic pile of pink, plastic poop into a paper disposable diaper. . . . Noah entered with a paperback book on international toycraft. "The child should be an artist, not a housewife!" he told her father, Angelo. . . . Pat Campley sat at the table dressed like Marilyn Monroe, eating cherries with a cordless plastic vibrating spoon. . . . Her mother, Sophia, kept running in and out with bowls of food and drying her red hands on her apron. . . . Zaddock Zinsburg was reciting a mantra over her cremating body. . . . Her Avocado Tree shared the funeral pyre with her. . . . They were both becoming ashes on the wind, which Oliver tried to catch and put into his pocket as he dusted crumbs from the tablecloth. . . . His face displayed an impenetrable anger. . . . Rosalie Steinbauer sat inside of a cornucopia combing her armpits as Narcissa Tittle sat beside her, poking a large dill pickle into the hole of a bagel. . . . Stanislaus played with dials that controlled the fire over which she roasted. . . . Juanita rattled the bars of her cell, weeping with hysterical laughter. . . . Dorissa floated through the redwoods like ashes on the wind. . . . She met up with a crucified Christ, who lay upon the knees of a blue-robed Virgin Mary. . . . Mary pushed him from her lap and shouted, "Get up and live, Son, you're getting too heavy for me!" Then she took off her blue robe and began to belly dance in an ecstatic birth mime, pushing a female child out from between her legs as she squatted on the earth, rolling and rolling her belly. . . . Juanita rattled the bars of her cell, laughing and crying hysterically to be let out. . . . Dorissa tried to dance toward her, but burning coals scorched her feet as an electrode within her attracted TV cameras, which sent her ghost out over the land in video waves like psychic plasma. . . .

She woke in a sweat, not knowing, for an instant, where she was. She shook out her hair and rattled her head to get the nightmare images out of her mind. A faint beam of light fell through a crack in the drapes of her motel window. In the darkness, it lit the leaves of her Avocado Tree. She got up and drew the drapes, exposing a view of trees off on the horizon beyond the neon signs of the highway and the motel. She felt weak and spiritless as she rubbed the sleep from her eyes. In a few hours, Dorissa would be performing her ritual dance for Thanksgiving under those trees. The dawn sky was dark and foreboding. She stroked the leaves of her Avocado Tree. Its voice spoke to her subliminally. "All prophets must go insane before they are free to serve sanely. Go alone to the forest and dance to the ancient trees!"

As the first light of dawn filtered down through the gray mist that shrouded the tops of the giant redwoods, Dorissa backpacked her Avocado Tree's terrarium along a deserted path. She looked up, her eyes brimming with the sight of the incredible trees that had grown for centuries along the gentle humid Pacific Coast. Beneath their evergreen branches, she walked through delicate ferns unveiling their fronds from deep humus, through patches of pink-flowered oxalis, red alder, many-colored azalea and rhododendron. Now and then a deer or a salamander, a bird or a mole, scurried or fluttered across a shady grove. The anxiety created in her by her nightmare, just a little while earlier, began to melt from her as she wandered through the filtering light of the forest dawn. Contemplating natural antiquity, she thought of the indomitability of the redwoods, which had stood like cathedrals, outlasting disease, fire, ice, and lightning for centuries. Ashamed of how she was having trouble getting through one life span, she breathed in the damp vegetable smells and felt the peace and seclusion of the vast and ancient wood.

Finally, she arrived before the giant cornucopia, where she was to dance that afternoon. In the dawn hour, the spot was deserted and the fruit display covered with a huge gray tarpaulin. Taking the Avocado's terrarium off her back, she opened it and placed the small tree alongside the tallest of the gigantic redwoods. Ignoring the morning chill, she removed all of her hiking clothes and stretched out flat on the fern-covered Earth, gazing directly up the trunk of the huge tree. "Please give me your wisdom!" she implored. Spiritual fervor combined in her with a sense of human failure, causing a cascade of tears to issue from her eyes.

Finally, there in the desolate dawn hour, she rose to her feet and began dancing to the natural sounds of chirping birds, rustling leaves, and crackling twigs, praying as if in a trance to the trees. She portrayed an ecstatic birth in which she imagined herself pushing out from between her own legs. She spun around like a whirling dervish lost in a trance, moaning and laughing and crying, for what must have been a very long time, because when Stanislaus arrived in his Parks Department Jeep, loaded with sound equipment for the rehearsal, she was still spinning. As he walked toward her, he noticed that her eyes were glazed and her hair wild. She seemed to turn effortlessly, as if moved by some force beyond her. When she didn't respond to him, he became alarmed. He stepped up to her and grabbed her by the shoulders. She collapsed in a heap in his arms. He shook her awake. Suddenly his face snapped into focus before her.

"You were moaning and laughing and spinning faster than I've ever seen you do. I think you were dancing in your sleep. You're cold as ice. The sun hasn't come out today either. Maybe you can give California a boost in the solar plexus!" Dorissa didn't answer.

She just stared into his face. He took off his jacket and wrapped it around her. "Here, you're shivering," he said, beginning to rub her back vigorously.

She finally whispered hoarsely. "That feels good. Your hands are absolutely angelic! I didn't sleep very well!"

"You've been pushing and now everything's accomplished and you're collapsing a little. I sensed it last night when you came to my room. Your aura was low and your energy down."

She submitted her aching body to his hands. She was only half awake and more exhausted than she'd ever been. As he massaged her into warmth, her arms went up around his neck, and she found herself kissing him firmly on the mouth.

He pulled back a little in surprise. They gazed into each other's eyes. His hands crept up under the denim jacket he'd wrapped her in and ran over her back and breasts. She found herself becoming sexually excited for the first time in months.

"I've been wanting you to kiss me like that!" he said, "like a woman kissing a man. All this time I've been massaging you and you've just been lying there like a female chauvinist, never offering to massage me in return, just rolling over and snoring when I was done."

"But I thought I was doing what you wanted me to—increasing my aura and energy, relaxing totally, letting my feelings go while controlling my actions, like you said!"

"I wanted to turn you on so you couldn't resist me, but you've resisted me just fine, until now. It's probably been the longest foreplay in history! I wanted so much for you to ask me to fuck you."

Dorissa was confused and more awake. Immediately, her other lovers came to mind. They'd expected her to be part of their own private schemes. "What are you after, Stan—sex, money, or both?"

"I'll tell you the truth. I've been using Femfunelli, Inc., as a front for my own little scheme. While we've been traveling around the country, I've been secretly tapping my way into Ma Bell's telephone system and zapping a subliminal signal through the Pentagon's black box."

"What are you talking about? Whose box?"

He explained to her that the Pentagon had a powerful radio signal reserved for national emergencies. By vibrating his voice at an infinite number of megacycles per second, he could make it bypass the ear and enter the brain, directly. He'd figured out how to zap his own voice across the land via the Pentagon's powerful signal. He planned to be the subliminal voice of the nation. "I can even create an atomic explosion with sound!" he laughed a little maniacally.

She noted the gleam in his satanic eyes. "You scare me! You sound like a dangerous technocrat!"

"All scientific genius is potentially dangerous. Remember, even the gentle Albert Einstein, humanitarian that he was, helped to build the atomic bomb. That's the trouble when politicians get ahold of scientific truth! I served in the Korean War. Radioed helicopters. I saw at close hand what bombs can do!" He lowered his head in despair. "Now that I'm zapped into the Pentagon's signal and can tell this country anything I want to, now that I hold the power in the palms of my hands, I don't know what to do with it. I keep thinking of all those children and women and men out there who can hear me, and I don't know what to say."

"Just like a technocrat! You get your logic in advance of your *feelings!* The reason I've never kissed you before is you're always so damned cool and logical."

"That's not true! There's a lot of feeling in my hands when I touch you! Just because I haven't grabbed you and fucked you, you think I've got no feeling for you. You women are all alike. You only expect one thing from a man, a great romantic fuck that's going to send you to paradise, a flawless knight, a prince charming who takes you away to a dream castle, forever."

"It's just like a technocrat to want to be the subliminal voice of Big Brother! Your subliminal signal is no better than a gun. You are outrageously immoral!"

"Look who's talking about immorality! The media messiah, herself, a mixed-up feminist religious freak!"

"I don't claim to be any messiah! I'm just a prophet of Mother Earth's Second Coming! You're a mad technocrat, a sound freak! You've been using me for your technocratic power game! You're as bad as Delila and Noah and Pat—even worse, because you're more deceptive. It's one thing to be a prophet, if you feel called. It's another to be carried away with your own mad genius! What incredible egotism, to want to be the subliminal voice that broadcasts throughout the country!"

"You're right. That's why all I've said so far is, 'Testing, one, two, three, testing!'" He bit his lip. "I keep thinking of all those people out there who will hear me the way a fish hears in water, with their bodies. I realize I could have everyone in the palms of my hands, and I don't want them. All I want is you. I realize I've been making love to you with my electrodes and machines because I want to make love to you with my body. That's why I got so upset that night, on Delila's terrace, just before we left New York, when you were playing tantric hanky-panky with Zaddock Zinsburg, that saintly poet!"

"Saintly poets are harmless compared to freaky scientists like you!" She walked away from him.

"Please don't. I fell in love with you that night when you resisted Delila, Pat, and Noah and went on this tour despite their hoity-toity ambitions, and the fact they refused to mention. This tour is peanuts compared to what you could be making now in Europe. I like your pluck. My wife was lily-livered and materialistic when it came to stardom. She wanted it for her insatiable insecurities. She never believed I really loved her because I didn't act like a prince charming. She needed constant approval from her audience. But you, you forget yourself completely and try to give them something. I've given plenty of orgone massages, but I haven't gotten into any serious heterosexual loving for years! I dug you! But I've been a celibate ever since my wife left me!"

"You know what I think, Stan? I think you're afraid of emotional involvement, afraid of just being used for your mind."

"The CIA wanted to recruit me when I was in college, scoring high on my College Boards, tops in the country! I opted for a career in sound engineering because music seemed harmless enough."

"Your wife took advantage of your genius to make herself a star! That's probably what you think I would do."

"What's the use? I'm not even sure I could fuck you if I tried.

I'd probably be impotent after all this time!" Stanislaus' eyes watered with tears.

Dorissa's heart went out to him. They sat across from each other beneath the giant trees in Full Lotus, gazing into each other's eyes, as in the first position of Yab-yum Tantric yoga.

"All these months I've been busting my ass working for you, I've never given a damn for your fame or money. It's that innocent way you have of really believing, like a child, in what you're doing. It makes me want to help you. I've been following myself around, saying I want to use Femfunelli, Inc., for my black-box scheme. All because I didn't want to believe you were the reason I was sticking around. I got myself zapped into the power, and I didn't know what to say!"

"I know how you feel. I've got all this media power, and I don't know where to take it from here. My lawyers say Oliver is coming around to settling out of court. I'm sure I'll be able to keep Chrysta now, but I wanted to go around this country for other motives, too. It's all got to do with the Great Goddess, *the feminine principle of psychic feeling* in men and women that makes them *feel* what's right. Noah says Carl Jung writes all about it! I mean this country is a mess, but it's my home. My parents came here steerage passage from Italy because they really wanted to be here. My father worked like a dog to be what he thought was a respectable *American!* I know Europe is full of gorgeous art and ancient culture, but where else could a peasant immigrant's daughter become a big media personality like me? Where else could I be the belly-dancing priestess of feminism but here? *And all overnight!*

"You know, priestess, I haven't wanted to tell you this, but there's no exact, 100 per cent, scientific way of proving that you are really communing with Earth through your Avocado Tree. I know I'm zapped into the Pentagon, but I'm not exactly sure I'm really zapped into you!" He looked guilty with the confession. "It may just be your pazzaz that's doing it!"

"Stan, I don't care what you say. I know my pazzaz comes from my solar plexus. The Great Goddess wisdom comes through me when I'm blabbering on those talk shows. I always know just what to *say* for Her. But I don't exactly know what's the right ecological thing to *do* for Her. I don't know what to do with all this media power, or what to invest my assets in. I feel like a turkey roasting on a platter. I couldn't sleep. I had nightmares all night!" She began to weep a little, as he had earlier.

Her arms went up around his neck, and his went around her back. They held each other close.

"You know when I like you best, priestess?"

"When?" she sniffled.

"When you're out there dancing. You're completely alive in the moment, sheer orgone energy! I can even see the aura emanating from you!"

"I just get lost in feeling!"

"I know. *Feeling* is what it's all about! Like right now. When I touch your breasts, like this! Whatever your mission, whatever mine, we're two mortals, caught for a scant moment in the flux and flow of the infinite universe, coursing with cosmic energy!" He sighed.

They saw each other in their eyes. They felt like one self looking out through both. The conceptual boundaries between their bodies disappeared. They realized that they were two separate halves of a whole, capable of the great primordial love that makes the world go around. They felt a deep trust in each other. It was sheer feeling, not at all intellectualized. Dorissa began undressing Stanislaus until he was naked as she.

"I've been waiting for you to notice that I was a man and not just a mind for Femfunelli, Inc."

"I always thought you were a cynical loner all wrapped up in your machines, a flaky genius devoid of human passions!"

As they sat across from each other in Full Lotus, his stamen began to rise toward her pistil.

"Look, Stan. There's a ladybug in your pubic hair! *Mamma mia*, there's three of them!"

"I passed through some grape groves on the way here!"

"It's a sign from the Earth Mother that she approves!" She reached out, picked a cluster of oxalis and a fern frond, and placed them in his dark brown curls.

He needed little encouragement to continue the ritual adorn-

168

ment. He picked a delicate white flower, tickled her nipples with it, and placed it in her pubic curls.

She leaned forward, taking his face in her hands, and kissed him on the mouth.

"You know," he responded, "you could try sponsoring the six-o'clock news with live nests of ladybugs to discourage the use of pesticides. You could invest capital in ladybug breeding!"

She buried her face in his neck. "That's a terrific idea!" She inhaled his male odor.

He sighed and inhaled her female odor. "You could even get all the women in America to turn in their toasters, recycle them, and use the money for a campaign against plutonium waste pile-up!"

"I could make it a fashionable moral issue not to eat toast and save a whole lot of electrical fuel power at the same time. After all, what's toast? Let them eat bread!"

"You could make untoasted toast even more fashionable than Cher's fingernails and change the course of nuclear civilization! There's a toaster in practically every home in this land!"

"And there's a TV set, too!" His enthusiasm for her work thrilled her. It turned her on, totally. She tickled his nipples, slowly climbing into his lap. Then she maneuvered her yoni downward over his lingam. He lightly pinched her nipples and stroked the bud of her yoni which erected to his touch.

"You are my cosmic other half."

"There's so much work we could accomplish *together*, so many hungry children we could feed."

Their eyes watered, and not just with pleasure anxiety.

"Priestess, I don't know if you realize it, but the mania of your Earth worship belly dance is spreading like wildfire throughout the land. It's outdoing tennis, jogging, yoga, and Ti Chi! It's dropped Air Force Isometrics to the bottom of the charts."

"Really? I'm always too busy performing and being interviewed to tune in on all the feedback. I depended on Delila, Pat, and Noah for that."

"Do you realize you have the power to make it fashionable to live as *au naturel* as possible?"

"Stan, I think I'll make my slogan, 'Food you are and into food you shall return.' That way I'll altar the *dust* of patriarchal

169

religion into something more matriarchal and Earthy. Dust is so abstract! People should see how they've actually fertilized each other's bodies down through the ages!"

"Right. E=MC²!"

"You know, Stan, you really turn me on to *thinking!*"

"You really turn me on to *feeling!*"

"I could rid the cities of domestic dog shit by making it fashionable to belly dance barefoot in the streets!"

"You could do a barefoot tour of the big cities, next, and promote urban ecology!"

"I could stage a countrywide belly-dancing demonstration against plutonium waste! I could get Seth Raider, champion of consumer rights, to help me!"

"We could set up a Whole Earth Institute and satisfy Delila's jet-set bug by hobnobbing with famous naturalists all over the world! We could award research grants and even get into cancer research! I have a feeling my pyramid orgone treatments are a cure for cancer when combined with sound-enduced euphoria. The psychic healers all agree that cancer is bad vibes, combined with radiation, in the nervous system. I'm sure orgone energy is the neutralizer of atomic energy. That's why things that are given the feeling of love grow better, stay healthier.

"Stan, you'll have to give up your voice of 'Big Brother' scheme. It's too immoral and insidious!" She French-kissed him. "If you want to stick with me, you'll have to put feelings before technology!"

"I'll tell you what I'll do. I'll broadcast your dance ecstasy. I'll zap you into your Avocado Tree and send its vibes out over the land through the Pentagon's black box. Every time you roll your belly and enjoy it, so will everyone else, until the whole country dances with you for the sheer joy of it! If everybody gets his rocks off, maybe they'll have time to pay attention to what's good for them. Ecological truth! Not capitalist greed!"

"No thanks, Stan. Let me do it my way, with plain pazzaz." She giggled, confessing one of her wildest fantasies: "I'd like to turn the Statue of Liberty into a shrine for Earth worship, a tabernacle of the belly dance. After all, America had the Pennsylvania shakers! Why not the New York shimmies? I'd like to strengthen the solar plexus of this whole country! Harness it's biophysical energy for the Earth Mother. I could teach people to be so thankful for their food, so grateful for *photosynthesis*, that vegetables would become more plentiful than money! I might even get to do an Earth fertility rite at the next presidential inauguration!"

"We could have a ball together!"

"Do you think it could work?"

"What?"

"Us."

"I don't know for sure. We'd have to work hard at it."

"Human relationships aren't easy, not really *intimate* ones!"

She was rubbing his stem, and he was tickling her bud. She still sat in his lap, his lingam in her yoni. Her arms around his neck. His around her back. Their breasts were pressed together as they gazed deeply into each other's eyes, experiencing the wordless sensation of their bodies in total contact. They listened to the rhythm of their mutual breathing, embracing motionlessly. They allowed the intensity of sensation to suspend all verbal and conceptual thought so that there was no longer any notion of desire or sexual intercourse or of trying to make anything happen other than what was. They experienced a yogic transcendence of their worldly personalities and felt like a primordial pair, the Moon and Sun in syzygy. His lightning third eye opened the dark perfumed lotus of hers and they were one, like two halves of a Tibetan statue—a bronze image of a man and a woman that when fitted together exchanges the roles of sexual organs. Phallus becomes vulva and vulva becomes phallus.

They didn't move, didn't even try to come. They just looked into each other's eyes, breathing deeply. A family of tourists passed by. Just as the father remarked: "Look at those crazy naked beatnik hippies!" Stanislaus and Dorissa experienced total orgasm. Beneath the giant redwoods, their bodies and souls were for a moment in complete union. They'd discovered the really "Big O." Yin merged with yang in perfect balance.

Only minutes before her Thanksgiving television special, Dorissa sat in her tiny makeshift dressing room inside the giant cornucopia. The gray tarpaulin had been removed, and fruit, held in place by frail wooden scaffolding, poured forth onto the stage, where it ripened under many hot television lights, arranged on battens. There was a narrow walkway in the midst of the fruit through which Dorissa would make her entrance out onto the wooden platform, to be greeted by video cameras. She checked her costume, a skin-tight, flesh-colored body suit, cut out at the armpits, stomach, and feet, and hand-painted by body artist Chin Lo Slung. Instead of the green ferns and vines he'd painted on Dorissa in Woodstock, he'd encircled her belly with the biological symbol for female, a circle with a cross beneath. Around her breasts he'd painted red, white, and blue peace signs. She'd wanted to dance naked of her body suit, with just Chin Lo Slung's art decorating her skin, but FCC regulations prohibited her. She questioned the rules that made the human body taboo but allowed the gun to be ubiquitous on the nation's screens, but there was no changing them.

As she frizzed her hair, looking into her dressing-room mirror, she mused how she'd felt greater tenderness from Stanislaus, that afternoon, than from any lover she'd known, including Delila.

Aside from all reports by Kinsey, or Masters and Johnson, aside from all feminist or male chauvinist pig theories about sex, love, and liberty, aside from all theories about human sexuality, Dorissa Femfunelli instinctively knew there was one split second, one moment in time, when a woman feels, for sure, that she can love a man with her whole being. Nature supplied women with some very special, individual female nerves for feeling, for sensing the possibility of love at her very core. Because the moment a man's body enters hers, the very exact point in time at which his penis slides past her labia minora and up into her vagina to bump against her os, at that very point in time—if she stops to feel it— she knows, she understands, she senses from her toes to her crown the possibility or impossibility of true love for him. That moment is either a subtle orgasm of her entire body and spirit, the whole moist and juicy peach of her psyche, or it isn't. If it isn't, the most she will ever do with that man is be his mother or his sister, but his lover, his passionate devoted companion in life, never! Dorissa Femfunelli had felt such a moment with Stanislaus Yeski.

"If I keep trusting the feeling in his hands, I'll marry him. He seems to be after more than money or sex. I think he's after me, body *and* soul. But whatever happens," she resolved to herself, "my soul is going to be my own, and of course the Great Goddess who makes me *feel* what's right." In silent communion with her spirit, she stroked the leaves of her Avocado Tree and prepared to make her ritual entrance onstage. Outside before the cornucopia, several tourists and members of California's Board of Agriculture awaited her. The public-relations director of the redwood preserves had supplied folding chairs for her live audience. Televiewers in living rooms, kitchens, and bedrooms all over America awaited her, among them the avocado farmers of California. A gray, foreboding sky covered sunny California with its chill.

Suddenly, just a few brief moments before show time, Delila barged into Dorissa's dressing room through the back end of the cornucopia. She was immediately solicitous.

"Oh dahling, why didn't you answer my cards and letters, or receive my calls? I've been crazy with worry! Even though you've looked fine on the tube, I've missed you terribly!" She gave her superstar a long and lingering kiss on the lips, pressing her up against a pile of melons. In so doing she caused a small avalanche of fruit. Dorissa slid down on her back amid the melons. "You still turn me on like crazy!" sighed Delila, half lying on top of Dorissa. "Isn't this exciting, semiprivate sex amid juicy melons under the genius sequoia?"

Dorissa did not respond. Ever since Delila had kicked her Avocado Tree she'd lost all sensual feeling for her. She knew she could be excited only by someone who shared her concern for Mother Earth. She planned to change Femfunelli, Inc., to Earth Spiritual Industries, Inc., and make Stanislaus codirector with Delila. Among the two of them and Noah, she'd find the practical, aesthetic, and ecological way to invest her corporate assets. The idea had snapped together in her head as she made love with Stanislaus.

She tried to stand up. "Delila, let's get up. We're squashing all this fruit, and I'm having it donated to a local orphanage after the performance. Waste not, want not! Starving children could be eating it!"

"There you go with your *pleasure anxiety!*"

"It's not pleasure anxiety anymore, Delila, it's *social con-science!*"

"Oh dahling, I've come to make amends. Pat's phones have been ringing off their cradles ever since you did Yosemite. Every politician and businessman in the country wants you to do a benefit or a commercial. We've had to expand the office and install five more phone lines. Baby, you are it! They're starting to take you more seriously than they ever took Billy Graham, or the Maharishi of Transcendental Meditation. Marv Gavett wants you to do his show this week. He's offering a phenomenal sum, says he'll even go on location in the cornfields of Iowa for you.

"*Mamma mia*, Delila. It's good to have your feedback again. But I'll have to meditate on it."

"Meditate on it! What do you mean, dahling? It's thousands for an hour's work!"

"I'll do Marv Gavett if he'll use live ladybug nests as his sponsor."

"What are you talking about, dahling? I don't understand you."

"Just that I have a few ideas of my own about how I want to use my media power, Delila! But I want you to understand that I appreciate all you do for Femfunelli, Inc. You are a terrific manager!"

Just then Stanislaus, his black earphones atop his head, entered and half fell over Delila and Dorissa, still reclining in the fruit. Dorissa jumped to her feet as Delila rolled over to her side.

"What are you doing in the star's dressing room?" demanded Delila.

"You may as well know, Delila, I'm thinking of marrying Stan."

"What?" Delila felt challenged to a duel. She leaped up and swung her giant pocketbook at Stanislaus. "You cad, you stole her from me while my back was turned!" she shouted.

This time, Stanislaus was quicker than Delila. He grabbed her pocketbook before it hit its mark.

"Oh no, you don't! Not again!" he emitted. He held the pocketbook aloft. "This thing is heavy! What have you got in it this time?" He pulled a redwood carving of Isadora Duncan out of Delila's purse.

174

"It's a present for the priestess, to celebrate her triumphant tour! Thank God I didn't break it on your head!"

"How thoughtful and kind of you, Delila. *It's beautiful.* Now let me get ready to go on. I only have a few minutes."

Just then, Pat's voice came from the back of the cornucopia. "Priestess, honey, where are you? I want to give you a good-luck kiss before you go on!" He entered dressed in a suede miniskirt, stepped on a lemon with his wooden platform shoes and rolled to his back, exposing his pantyhose and upper thighs. "Goodness!" he squealed as he came down to Earth from his shoes, crashed into a pile of oranges, and caused an avalanche of grapefruit to fall on Stanislaus, who fell into Dorissa's lap just as Noah entered. Dorissa sympathetically clutched Stanislaus to her bosom as Noah announced:

"What's going on in here? The cameras are ready to roll!"

A pile of apples gave way and cascaded over Noah, who landed in Delila's arms as Pat tried to scramble to his feet in oranges. Delila suddenly realized she liked having Noah in her arms. "You're rather attractive, dahling," she said.

"*Madre mia!*" exclaimed Dorissa, falling back against Pat's pearls and upsetting his gray-blond Lord & Taylor wig. "I've got to go on, and you're all making a mess of me *and* the set!" She stood up, balancing precariously on a couple of watermelons to make a soapbox speech:

"Look, we have all got to get something straight! I became an artist of the dance with Noah's help and a superstar because of Delila's push. I made feminism into a spiritual movement for the Earth Mother because Pat encouraged me to worship the vulva. Stanislaus increased my aura with his orgone pyramid and my performance with his sensorized sound. But Juanita has taught me to hold onto my soul. My Avocado Tree inspires me, and the Great Goddess is the principle of femininity that I worship. She has taught me to trust my feminine feelings and intuition. I've risked everything, even Chrysta, to become the big media power that I am, and I want to do what is right with it. I began it all in one year, just like I promised myself in Aneera's studio mirror. I'm no crazy, mixed-up, helpless, hysterical nut anymore; I'm a woman, and my medium is my belly. I'm going to make it my message, too. So all of you get out of here right now, because I have to go on, this minute. The cameras are rolling." She scrambled off the watermelons out of the cornucopia followed by Stanislaus, who climbed over a pile of avocados to reach his soundboard. Delila, Pat, and Noah scrambled over lemons, oranges, and apples out after her, just as the back entrance of the cornucopia became blocked by an avalanche of fruits and vegetables.

Dorissa danced gingerly onto the stage followed by her wild entourage as the cameras began to roll in her direction. Stanislaus, as usual, flipped his switch, filling the redwood forest with sensorized sound.

Chrysta, back home in New York City, in front of Grandma's TV screen, joyfully spoke her mother's televised Thanksgiving Day prayer along with her. "Bless us, oh Mother Earth, for these your gifts that we receive from your American bounty, Ah women and men!"

Oliver, his face pinched, sat behind his daughter twiddling his thumbs. Since Dorissa's employment with the National Parks Service, his lawyers had suggested he settle out of court. There was no longer any chance of his proving that Dorissa was an unfit mother.

"Oh smile, Oliver, before your face cracks!" teased his own mother, giving him an affectionate pat on the cheek.

Dorissa's Aunt Raphaela called her Aunt Maria Domenica to make sure her set was on. She'd given up lighting candles to save Dorissa's soul. Uncle Giuseppi searched his wallet for Dorissa's baby picture so that he could proudly display it during his coffee break. Aunt Helena said seven "Hail Marys" in hopes that Dorissa would not be punished for changing the Catholic prayer of grace. Dorissa's mother, Sophia, wiped her eyes on the corner of her apron. "That's my baby on television!" she whimpered. Angelo Femfunelli smiled broadly as he sat in his slippers before the set. "She's a daughter, but she's good as a son!" he told his wife. Dorissa had immortalized his Italian name, and he was proud of her.

As Dorissa danced her greatest ecstasy, the newscaster made some esoteric remarks about the cornucopia, explaining it was an ancient fertility symbol for the female womb, pouring forth with

Earth's plenty. Then he noted that Dorissa Femfunelli, the shaman of feminism, had founded a neo-pagan spiritual movement throughout the country. "Homemade dumbeqs are replacing guitars on American campuses all over America!" he announced.

As Dorissa went into her ecstatic birth mime, the mischievous Stanislaus, forever bidding good-bye to his insidious black-box scheme, zapped her orgastic ecstasy into the Pentagon's power. Then ripped the subliminal switch from his soundboard. Her navel lit up the screen with telepathic aura. A circle of light like a belly button, for just one brief, imperceptible second, whited out all the screens across the land as umbilical waves of subliminal orgastic sound penetrated the atmosphere of Earth, caressing her television viewers in the flesh! Dorissa's smiling face lit the screens across the land as the sun came out over California. Radiant Earth felt like an amoeba having a cosmic orgasm in the waters of her own space. Her message was her medium.

Cultivate your own garden. Birth dance of Earth. Lift your seven green veils of Isis toward the Sun and Moon. Have orgasm as often as possible without neglecting your work, family, friends, or spiritual destiny. Save yourself for Earthsake.

Two Psalms by the Author,
Who Is a True Ritual
Celebrant
of
the Great Goddess Earth:

Read them as you roll your belly.

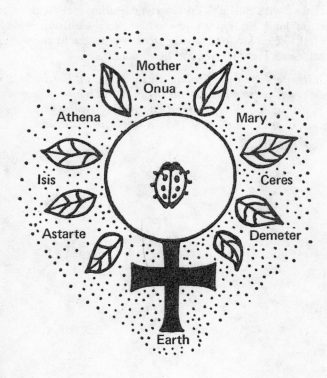

The Earth Is Feminine in Most Languages: A Psalm

(From an essential libretto for a new-world symphony)

—after a passage in the
Taittiriya Upanishad 2.2.

From food comes all, all that lives upon the Earth.
All is food, and to food it shall return.
Food is the only goddess among the living.

They are blessed with food who worship earth
for the Earth is food and goddess among the living.
All are born of food
and by food they grow.

The Goddess is Earth and food her panacea.
All are born of her food
and to food they shall return.
All eat Her
and She eats all.

Food you are
and to food you shall return.
That is why She is called Sugar! Blossom! Honey!

The Great Mother gave milk in the beginning
She arose as a dream from mud
but from Her comes food and from food: breath, spirit, truth,
worlds, and in works, immortality.

Belly Dancer

An Etruscan priestess
through whom the Earth speaks,
enters veiled; a mystery
moves toward the altar.
Unknown features, shadow of death, of brows,
of eyes, mouth, lips, teeth of the night,
jaw thrust forward like a pelvis,
navel hidden, mysterious circuit,
electrical plug of the first cries
thrust from the womb.
The silk covering hovers over her,
turns with a whirling gesture
round as the Moon that glows in her belly.
Her navel winks in an amorous quiver.
Amazing belly that stretches large enough
to let a life grow.
She glides, dips, shimmies,
thrusts one hip, then another
The music breaks. Pain
fills the drum. She
falls to her knees, doubles
over, leans back on her heels
as her stomach flutters, rolls
with contractions, upward, downward, sinks her head into the floor,
raises her pelvis, arching, widening.
Arms rise like serpents from a flesh basket,
beat, caress, nip, shimmer the air with rhythmic
pulse. At last
the bloody mystery emerges,
inch by inch the head presses

through the lost hymen.
Her grimace works into a smile.
The decked and bejeweled mother
pushes out her ecstasy.
The formless fluid shot into her,
molded, fired in the secret oven,
emerges, a child cries: It lives!
Its voice rings in her finger cymbals.

She rests her body, slowly
rises from the Earth.
Her breasts fill with milk.
She shakes them:
This is food, I am food.

Woman, whose nerve-filled clitoris
makes her shiver, ecstatic
mother, dance with a fury
around your circle of women.
Spin out the time locked in your own womb,
bloom from your uterus,
lady of the garden.
The Moon pulls you,
crashes waves on the shore.
Undulate the branches of your arms
in the wind, Goddess of Trees,
of all living things.
Your flesh is not defiled by
men who can't contain your mystic
energy of woman. Belly
that invites life to sleep in you,
breasts of mortal ambrosia,
Amazon groin that lit the hearth,
altar, oven, womb, bread
table, Earth
Mother, pagan
witch of magic birth,

from whom all suck
leaves that flow through the body's blood,
cave of your sex, our home,
Moon of Earth, Great Mother.